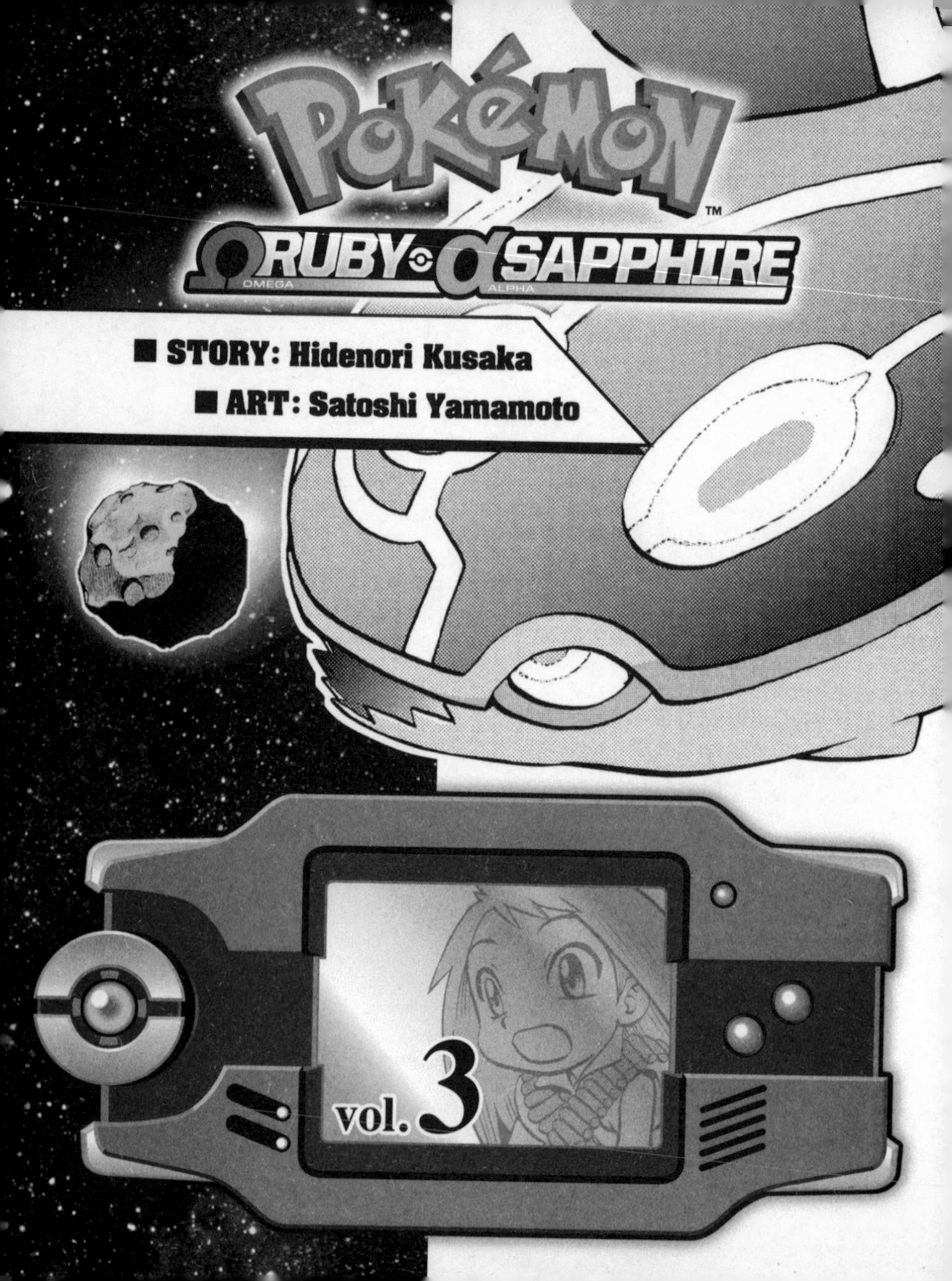
POKÉMON™
ΩRUBY·αSAPPHIRE
OMEGA
ALPHA
■ STORY: Hidenori Kusaka
■ ART: Satoshi Yamamoto
vol. 3

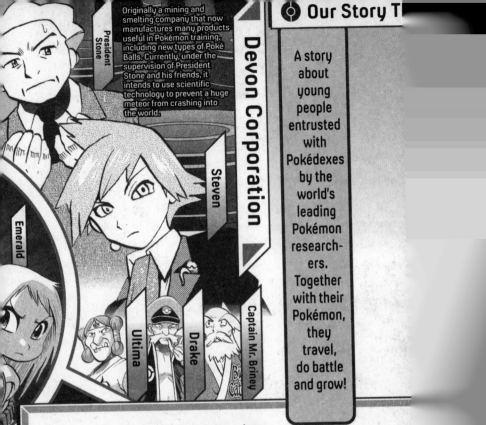

Our Story T

A story about young people entrusted with Pokédexes by the world's leading Pokémon research-ers. Together with their Pokémon, they travel, do battle and grow!

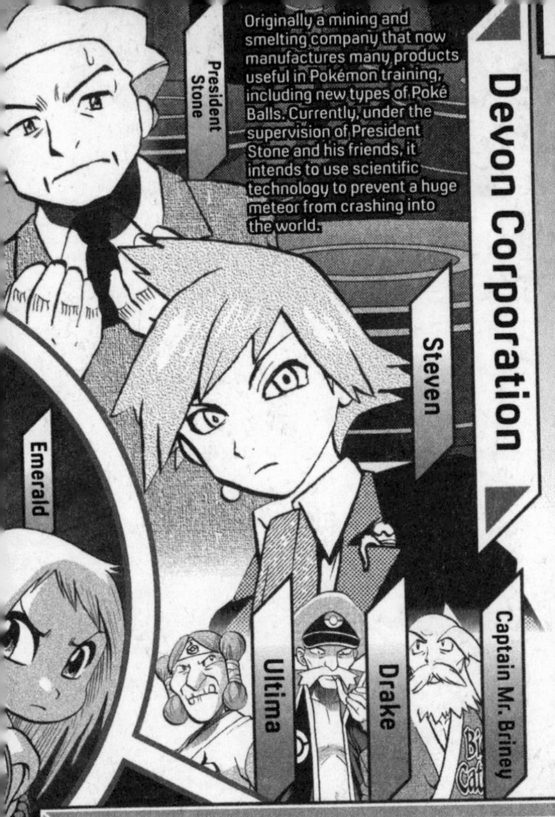
Devon Corporation
Originally a mining and smelting company that now manufactures many products useful in Pokémon training, including new types of Poké Balls. Currently, under the supervision of President Stone and his friends, it intends to use scientific technology to prevent a huge meteor from crashing into the world.
President Stone
Steven
Captain Mr. Briney
Drake
Ultima
Emerald

In order to power a machine to prevent a huge approaching meteor from striking the planet, Steven Stone, president of the Devon Corporation, summons the three Pokédex holders of Hoenn to help him convert the life force of many Pokémon into Infinity Energy.

Meanwhile, at Sky Pillar, Ruby is under attack from an angry Zinnia, the Lorekeeper of the Draconid people, who have long predicted the landfall of the meteor and claim they know how to prevent it.

Ruby decides to keep the news about the impending disaster a secret from Sapphire but is unable to make up his mind about whose plan to support. He learns from Zinnia that the key to stopping the meteor is Legendary Pokémon Rayquaza and a Trainer it trusts—which would be Ruby! So Ruby heads down to Sea Mauville to meet with Sapphire and the others while gathering more intel on Rayquaza...

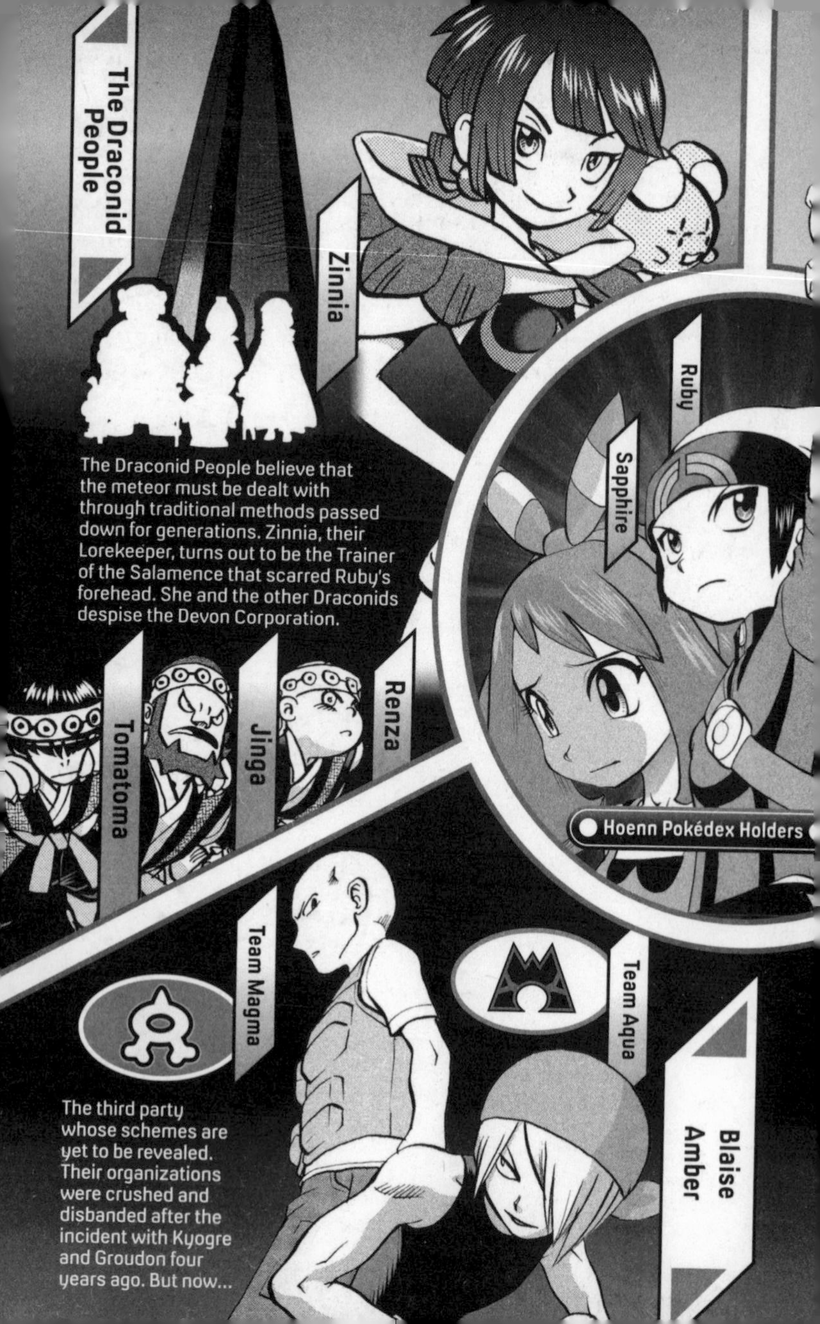
Zinnia
The Draconid People
Ruby
Sapphire
Hoenn Pokédex Holders
The Draconid People believe that the meteor must be dealt with through traditional methods passed down for generations. Zinnia, their Lorekeeper, turns out to be the Trainer of the Salamence that scarred Ruby's forehead. She and the other Draconids despise the Devon Corporation.
Renza
Jinga
Tomatoma
Blaise
Amber
Team Aqua
Team Magma
The third party whose schemes are yet to be revealed. Their organizations were crushed and disbanded after the incident with Kyogre and Groudon four years ago. But now...

CONTENTS

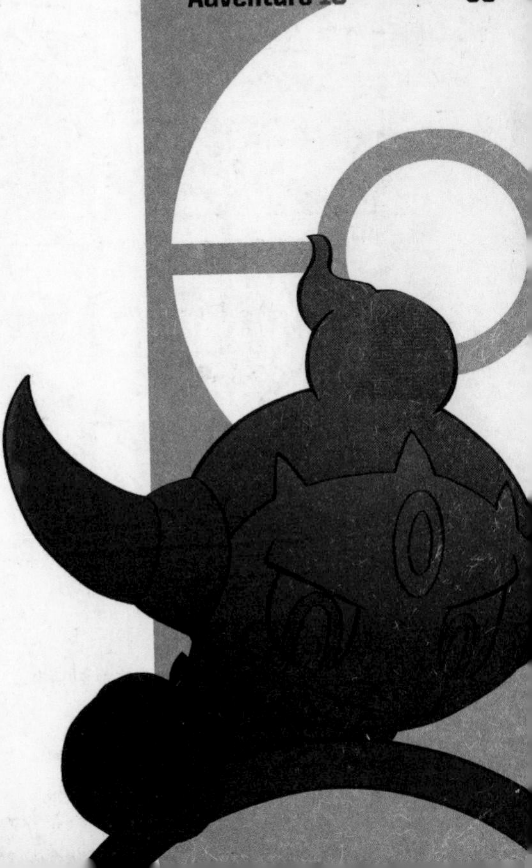

Omega Alpha Adventure 8

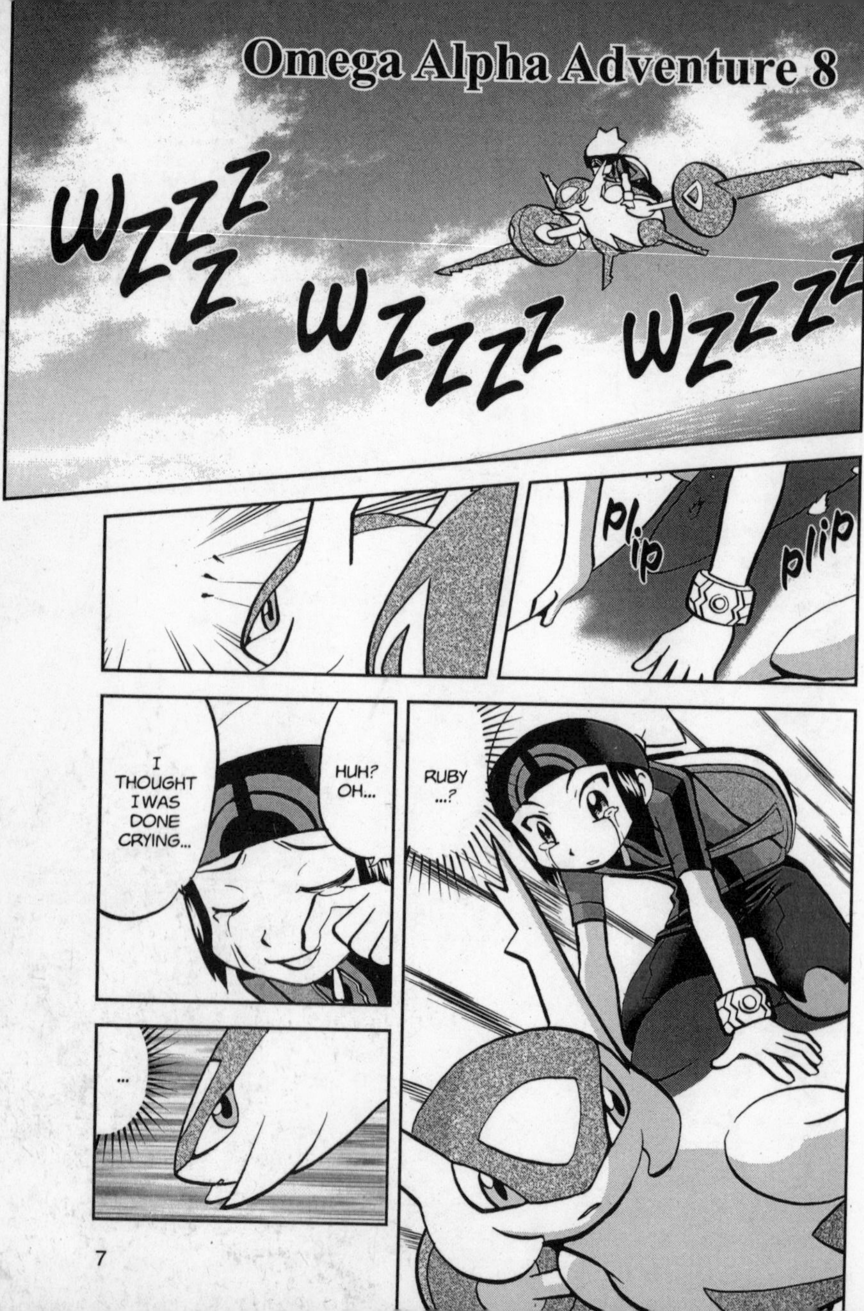
WZZZZZ
WZZZZZ
WZZZZ
plip
plip
RUBY ...?
HUH? OH...
I THOUGHT I WAS DONE CRYING...
...

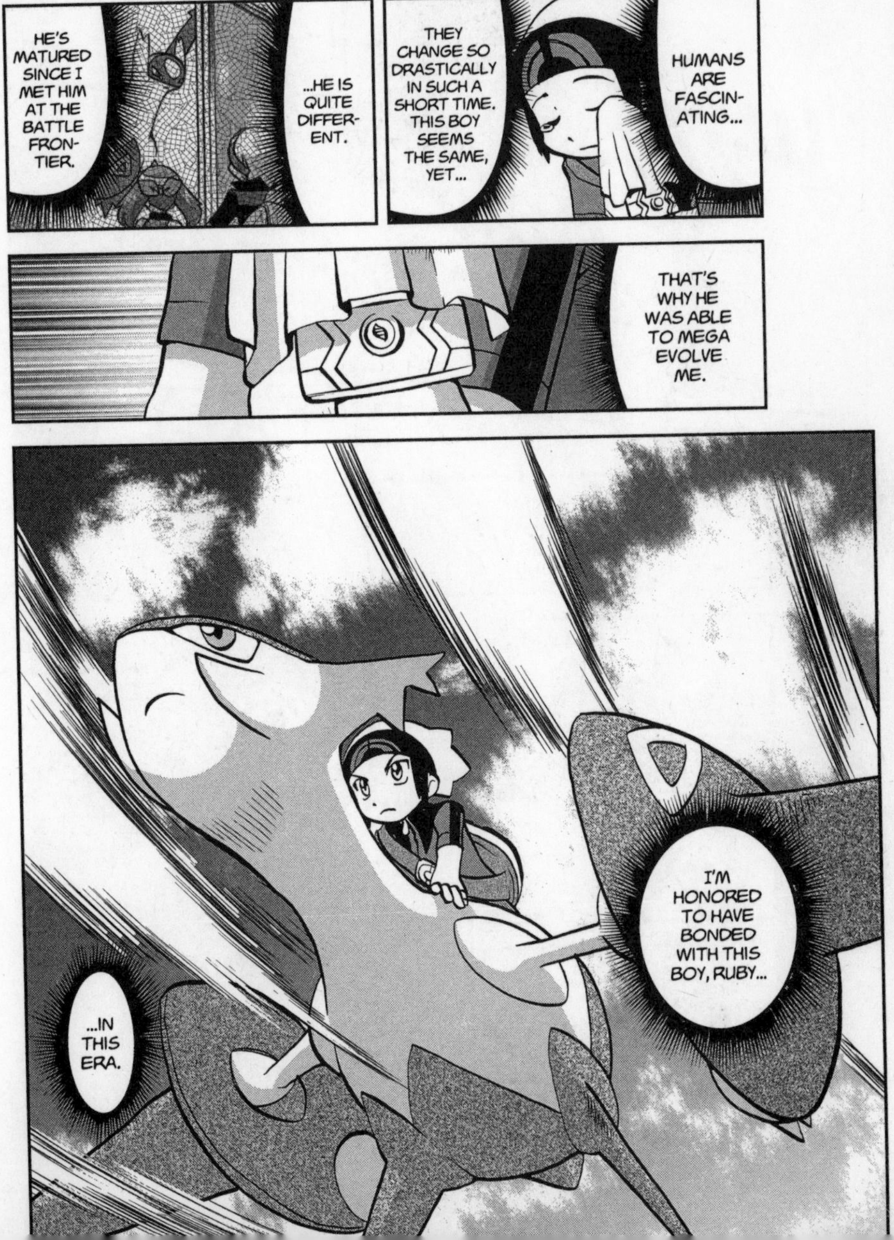
HUMANS ARE FASCINATING...
THEY CHANGE SO DRASTICALLY IN SUCH A SHORT TIME. THIS BOY SEEMS THE SAME, YET...
...HE IS QUITE DIFFERENT.
HE'S MATURED SINCE I MET HIM AT THE BATTLE FRONTIER.
THAT'S WHY HE WAS ABLE TO MEGA EVOLVE ME.
I'M HONORED TO HAVE BONDED WITH THIS BOY, RUBY...
...IN THIS ERA.

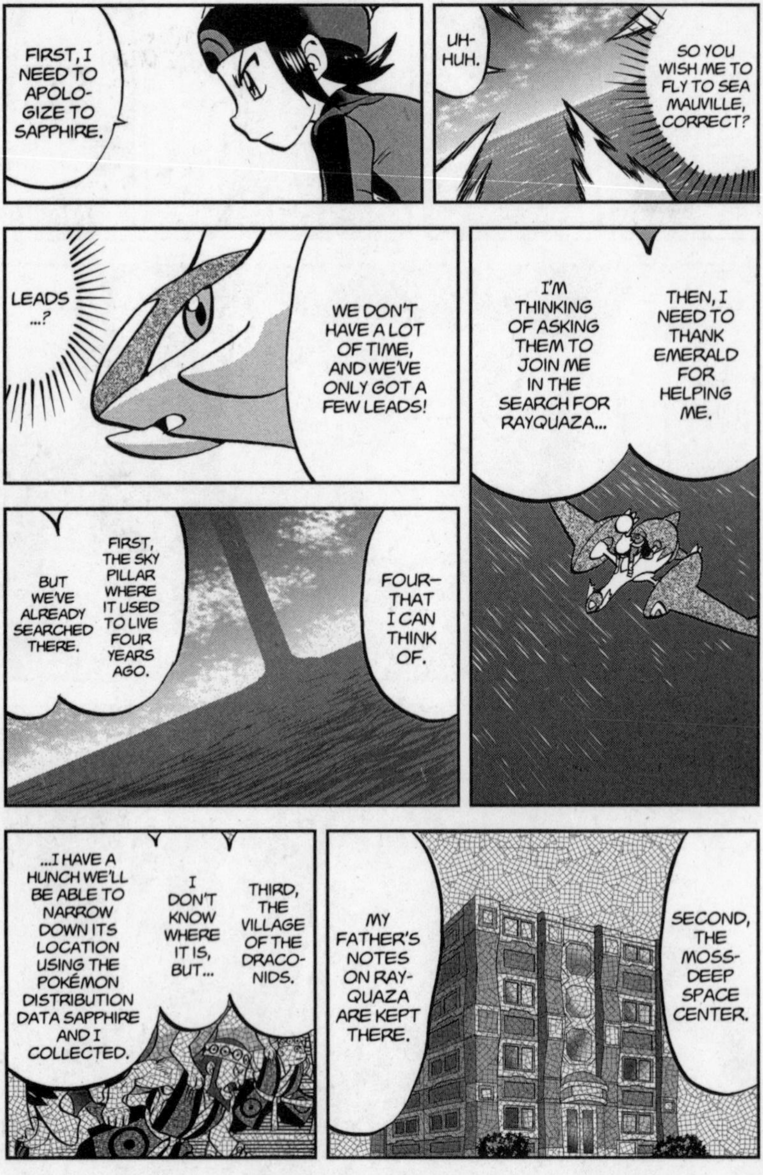
SO YOU WISH ME TO FLY TO SEA MAUVILLE, CORRECT?
UH-HUH.
FIRST, I NEED TO APOLOGIZE TO SAPPHIRE.
THEN, I NEED TO THANK EMERALD FOR HELPING ME.
I'M THINKING OF ASKING THEM TO JOIN ME IN THE SEARCH FOR RAYQUAZA...
WE DON'T HAVE A LOT OF TIME, AND WE'VE ONLY GOT A FEW LEADS!
LEADS ...?
FOUR—THAT I CAN THINK OF.
FIRST, THE SKY PILLAR WHERE IT USED TO LIVE FOUR YEARS AGO.
BUT WE'VE ALREADY SEARCHED THERE.
SECOND, THE MOSSDEEP SPACE CENTER.
MY FATHER'S NOTES ON RAYQUAZA ARE KEPT THERE.
THIRD, THE VILLAGE OF THE DRACONIDS.
I DON'T KNOW WHERE IT IS, BUT...
...I HAVE A HUNCH WE'LL BE ABLE TO NARROW DOWN ITS LOCATION USING THE POKÉMON DISTRIBUTION DATA SAPPHIRE AND I COLLECTED.

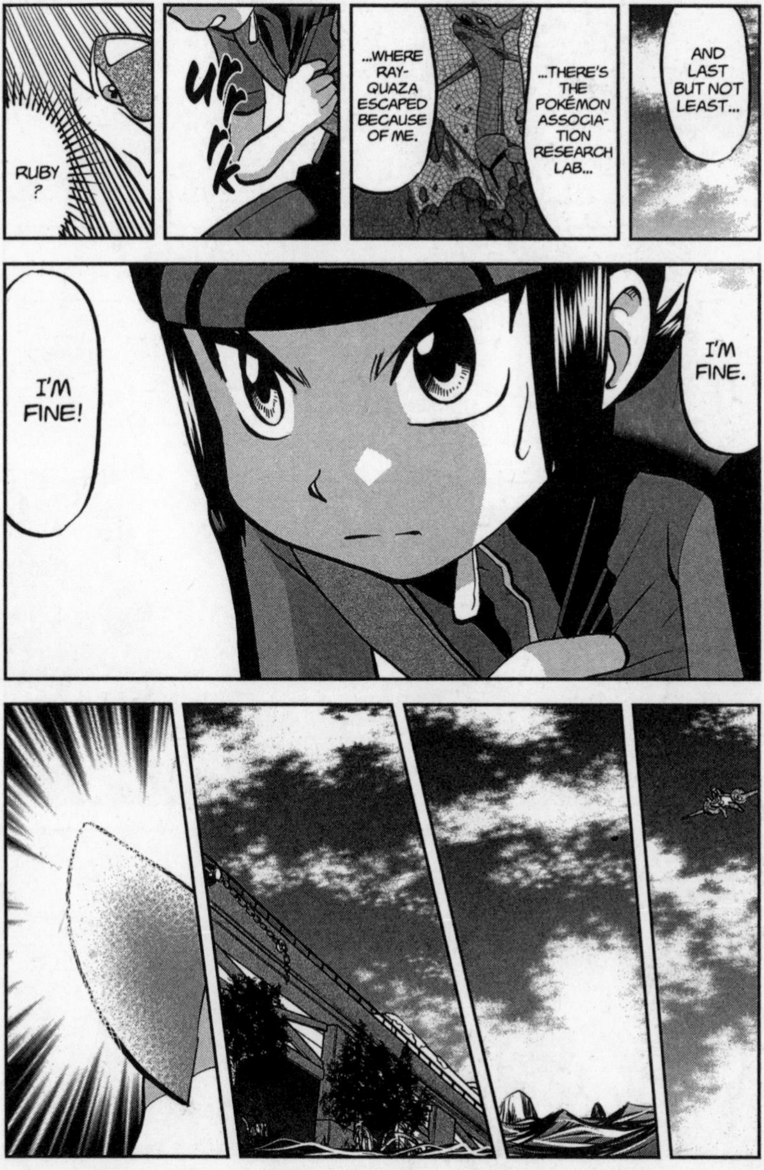
AND LAST BUT NOT LEAST...
...THERE'S THE POKÉMON ASSOCIA-TION RESEARCH LAB...
...WHERE RAY-QUAZA ESCAPED BECAUSE OF ME.
URRRK
RUBY?
I'M FINE.
I'M FINE!

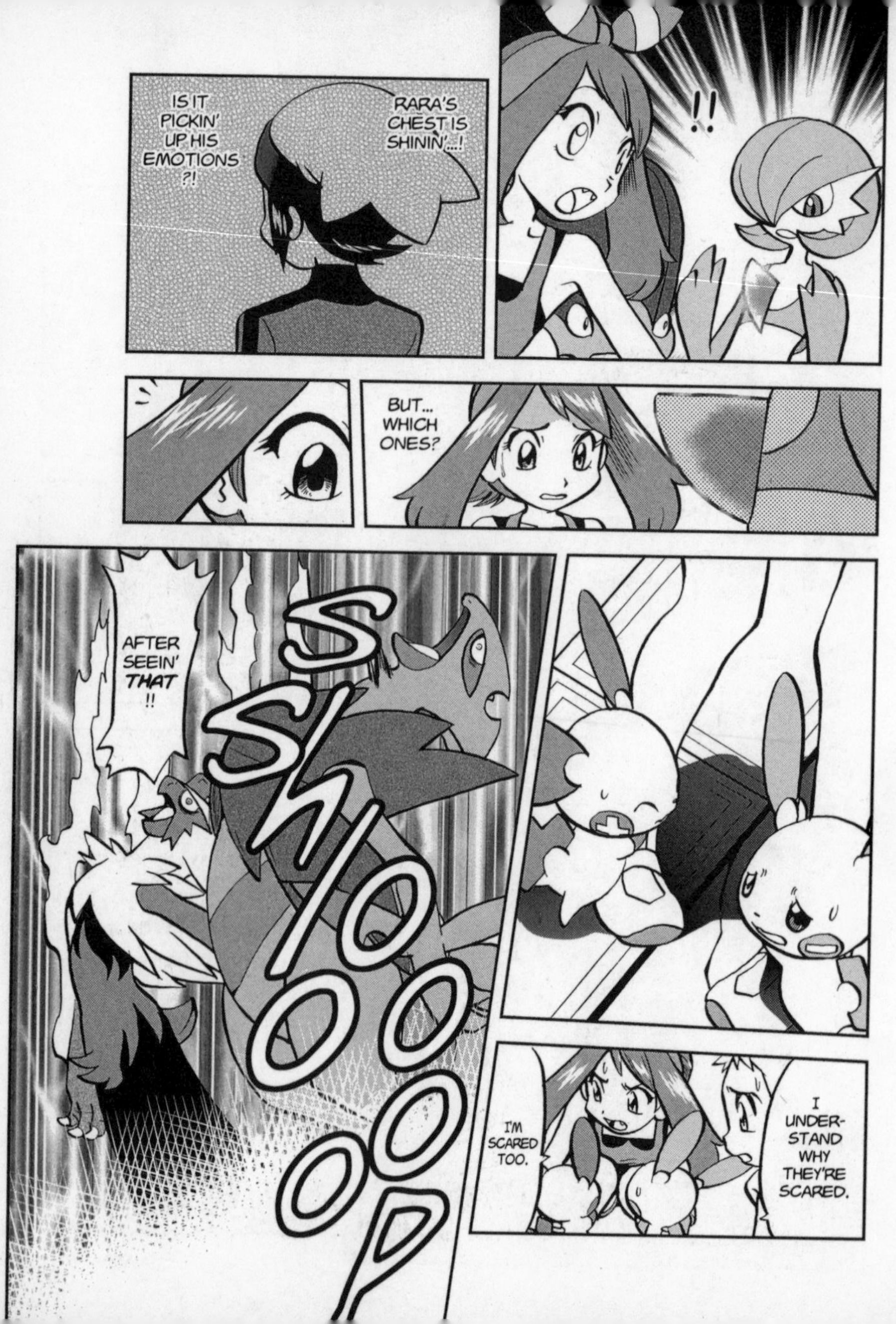
!!
RARA'S CHEST IS SHININ'...!
IS IT PICKIN' UP HIS EMOTIONS ?!
BUT... WHICH ONES?
I UNDER-STAND WHY THEY'RE SCARED.
I'M SCARED TOO.
AFTER SEEIN' *THAT* !!
SSHHOOOOOOP

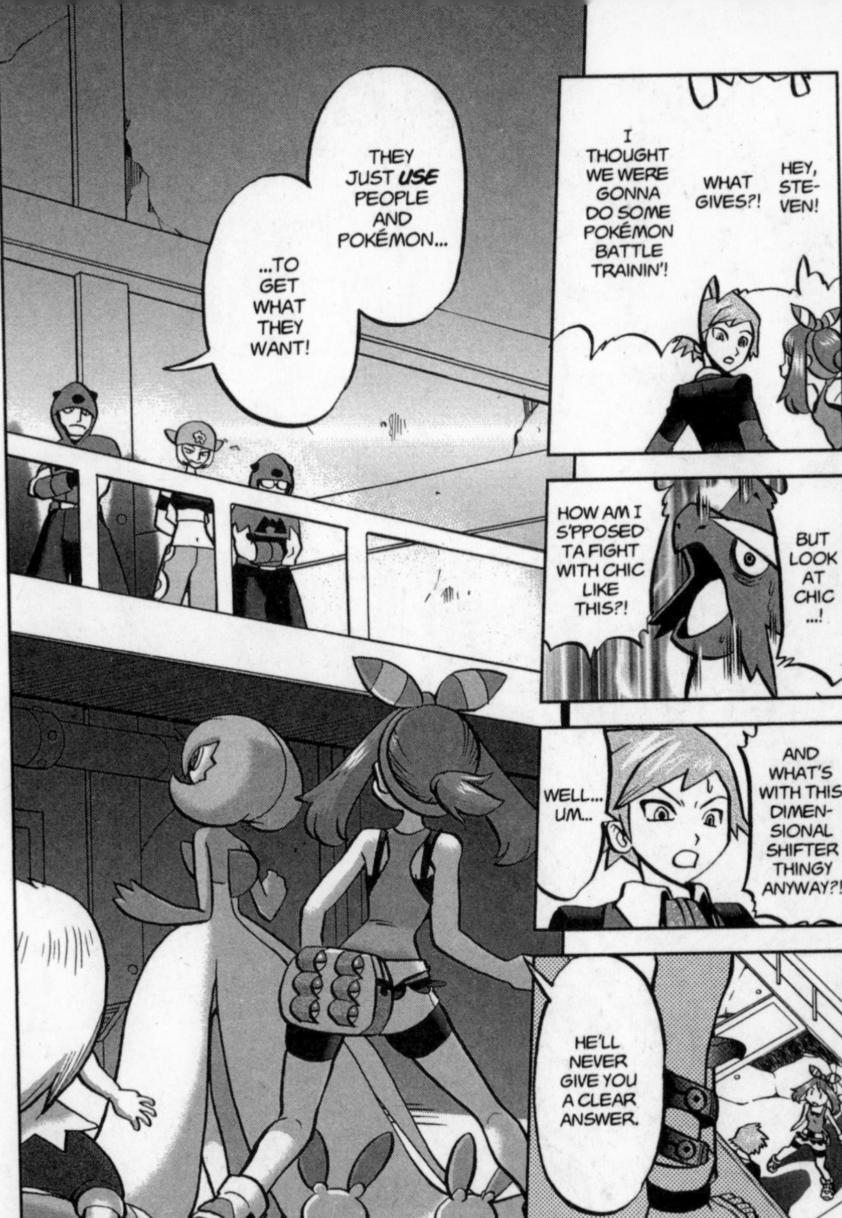
HEY, STE-VEN!
WHAT GIVES?!
I THOUGHT WE WERE GONNA DO SOME POKÉMON BATTLE TRAININ'!
BUT LOOK AT CHIC ...!
HOW AM I S'PPOSED TA FIGHT WITH CHIC LIKE THIS?!
AND WHAT'S WITH THIS DIMEN-SIONAL SHIFTER THINGY ANYWAY?!
WELL... UM...
HE'LL NEVER GIVE YOU A CLEAR ANSWER.
THEY JUST ***USE*** PEOPLE AND POKÉMON...
...TO GET WHAT THEY WANT!

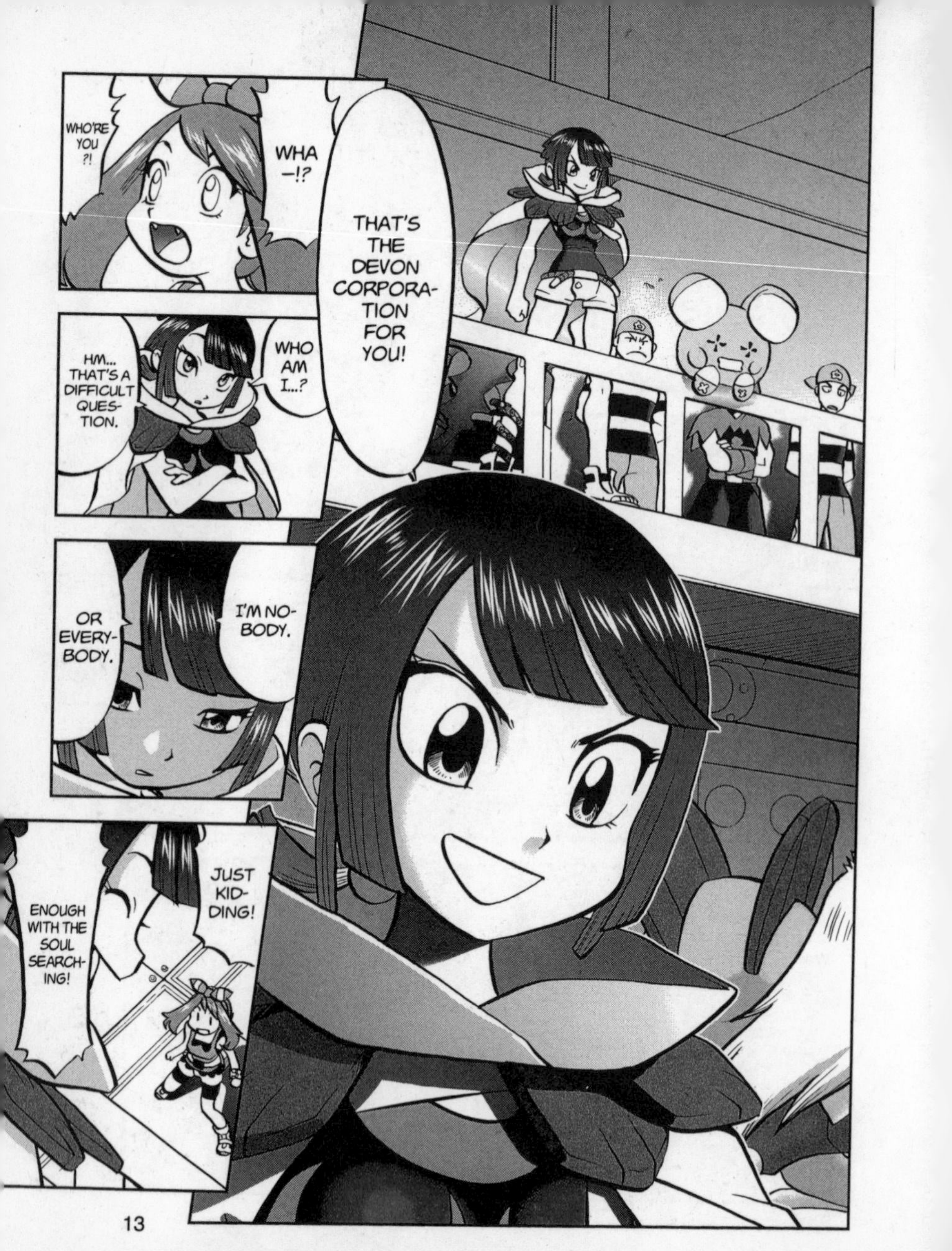
THAT'S THE DEVON CORPORATION FOR YOU!
WHA—!?
WHO'RE YOU ?!
WHO AM I...?
HM... THAT'S A DIFFICULT QUESTION.
I'M NOBODY.
OR EVERYBODY.
JUST KIDDING!
ENOUGH WITH THE SOUL SEARCHING!

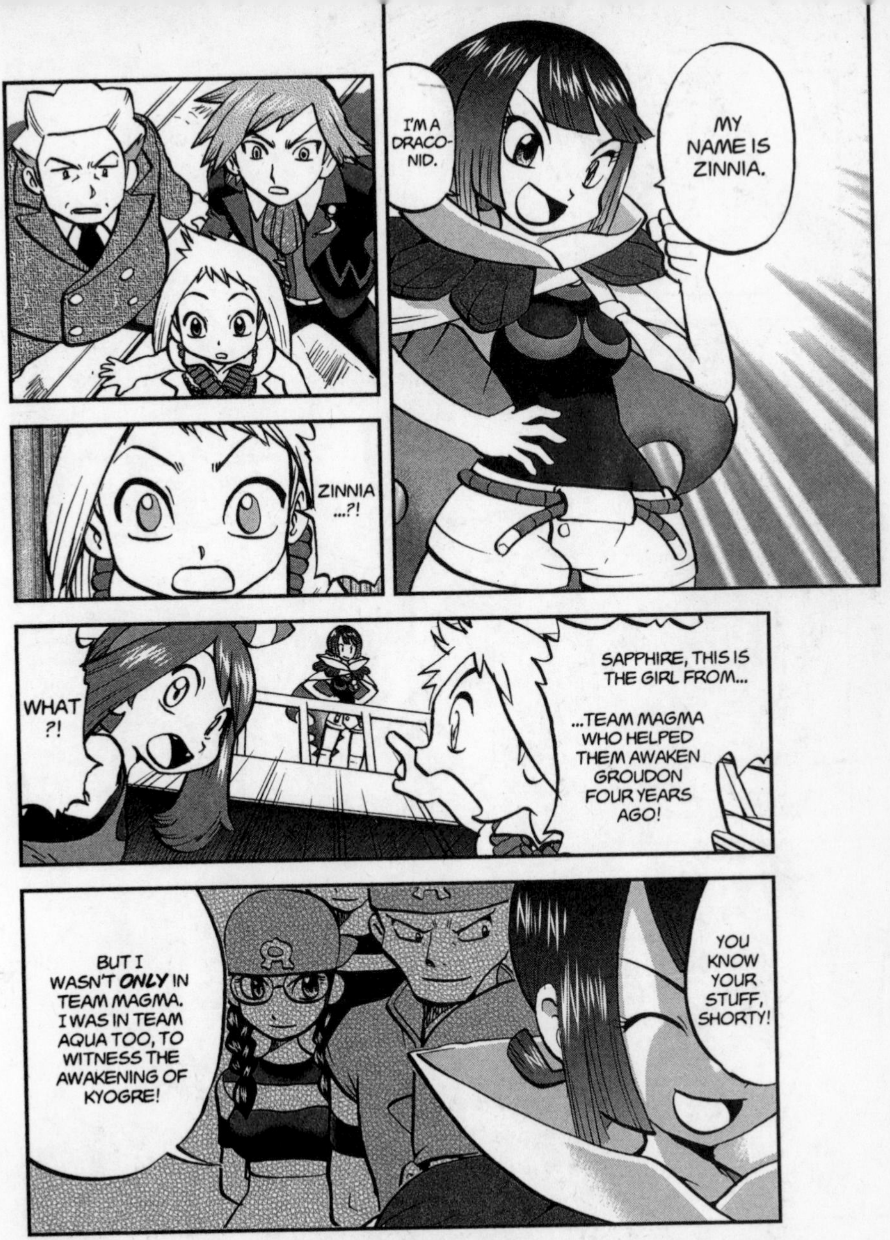
MY NAME IS ZINNIA.
I'M A DRACONID.
ZINNIA ...?!
SAPPHIRE, THIS IS THE GIRL FROM...
...TEAM MAGMA WHO HELPED THEM AWAKEN GROUDON FOUR YEARS AGO!
WHAT ?!
YOU KNOW YOUR STUFF, SHORTY!
BUT I WASN'T ONLY IN TEAM MAGMA. I WAS IN TEAM AQUA TOO, TO WITNESS THE AWAKENING OF KYOGRE!

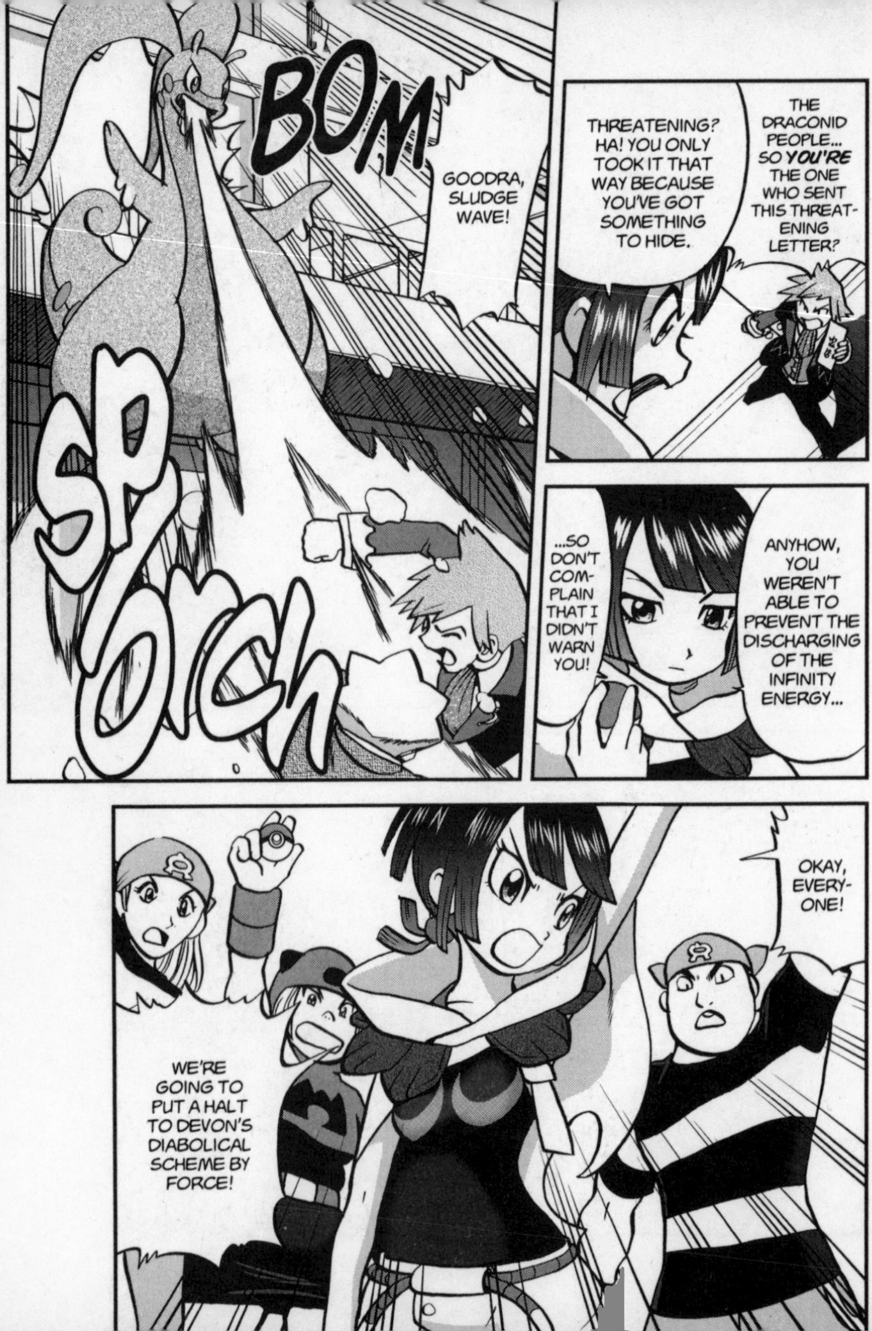
THE DRACONID PEOPLE... SO *YOU'RE* THE ONE WHO SENT THIS THREATENING LETTER?
THREATENING? HA! YOU ONLY TOOK IT THAT WAY BECAUSE YOU'VE GOT SOMETHING TO HIDE.
ANYHOW, YOU WEREN'T ABLE TO PREVENT THE DISCHARGING OF THE INFINITY ENERGY...
...SO DON'T COMPLAIN THAT I DIDN'T WARN YOU!
GOODRA, SLUDGE WAVE!
BOM
SPORCH
OKAY, EVERYONE!
WE'RE GOING TO PUT A HALT TO DEVON'S DIABOLICAL SCHEME BY FORCE!

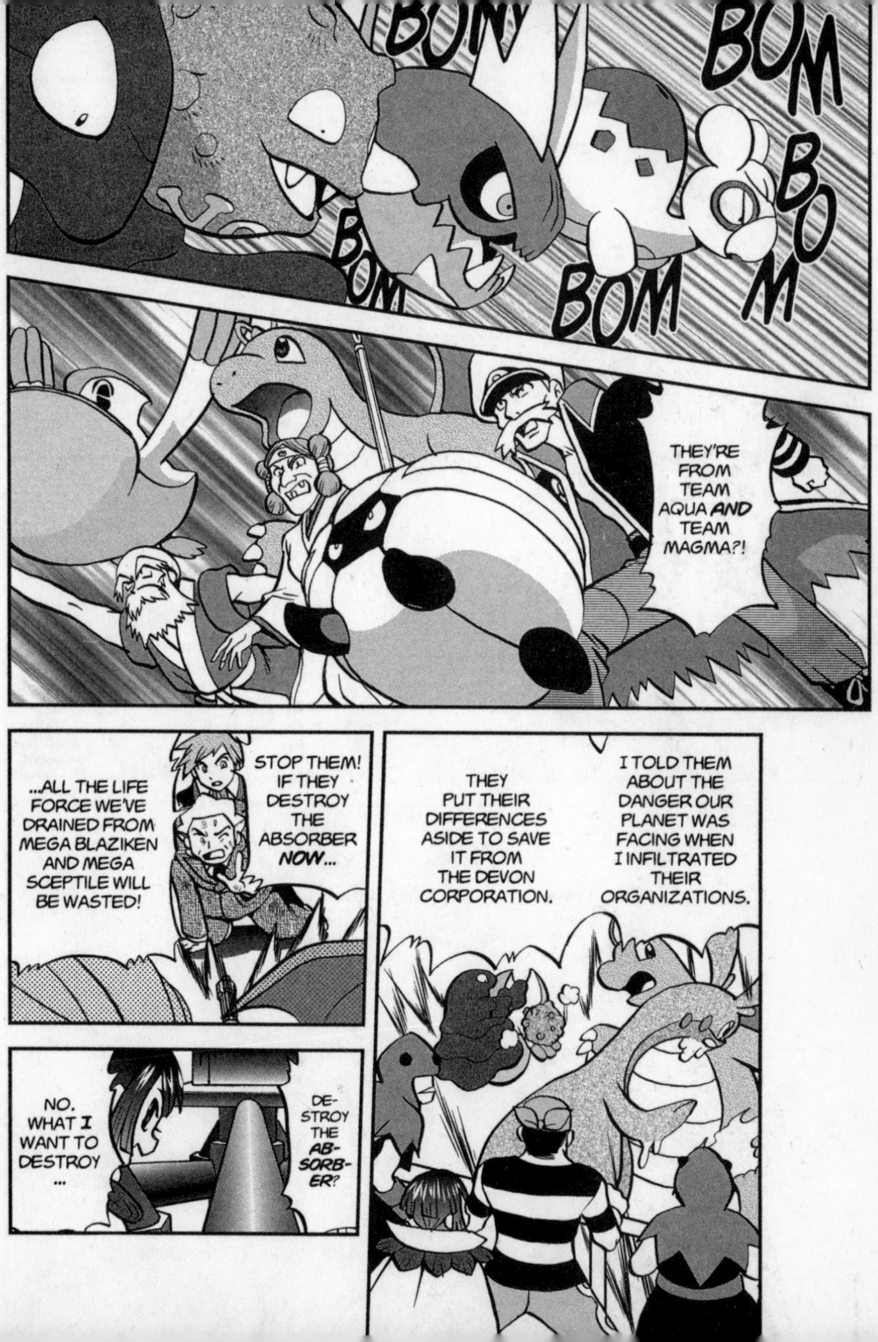
BOM
BOM
BOM
BOM
BOM
BOM
THEY'RE FROM TEAM AQUA **AND** TEAM MAGMA?!
I TOLD THEM ABOUT THE DANGER OUR PLANET WAS FACING WHEN I INFILTRATED THEIR ORGANIZATIONS.
THEY PUT THEIR DIFFERENCES ASIDE TO SAVE IT FROM THE DEVON CORPORATION.
STOP THEM! IF THEY DESTROY THE ABSORBER **NOW**...
...ALL THE LIFE FORCE WE'VE DRAINED FROM MEGA BLAZIKEN AND MEGA SCEPTILE WILL BE WASTED!
DE-STROY THE **AB-SORB-ER?**
NO. WHAT **I** WANT TO DESTROY ...

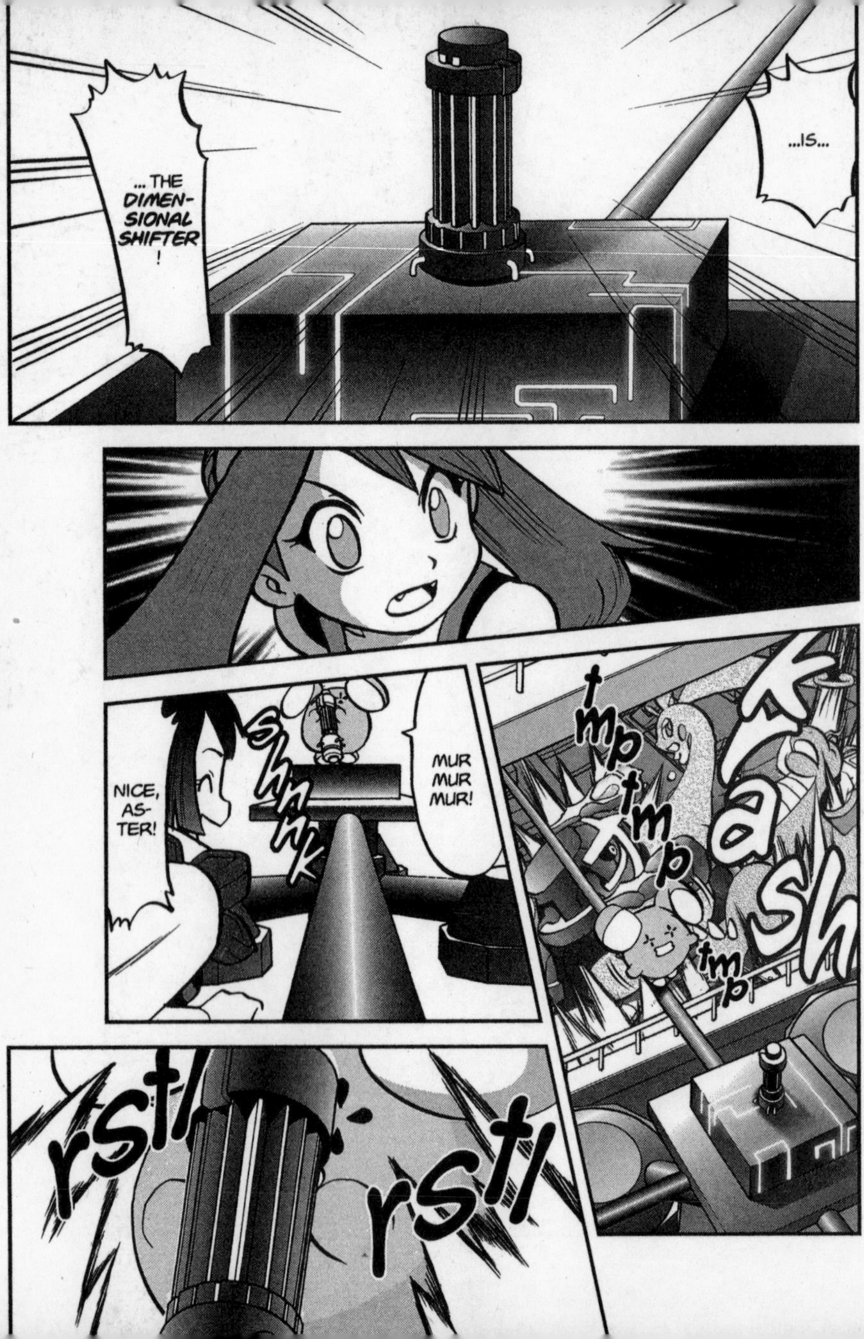
...IS...
... THE DIMENSIONAL SHIFTER!
kashh
tmp tmp tmp tmp
MUR MUR MUR!
shhnk
NICE, ASTER!
rstl rstl

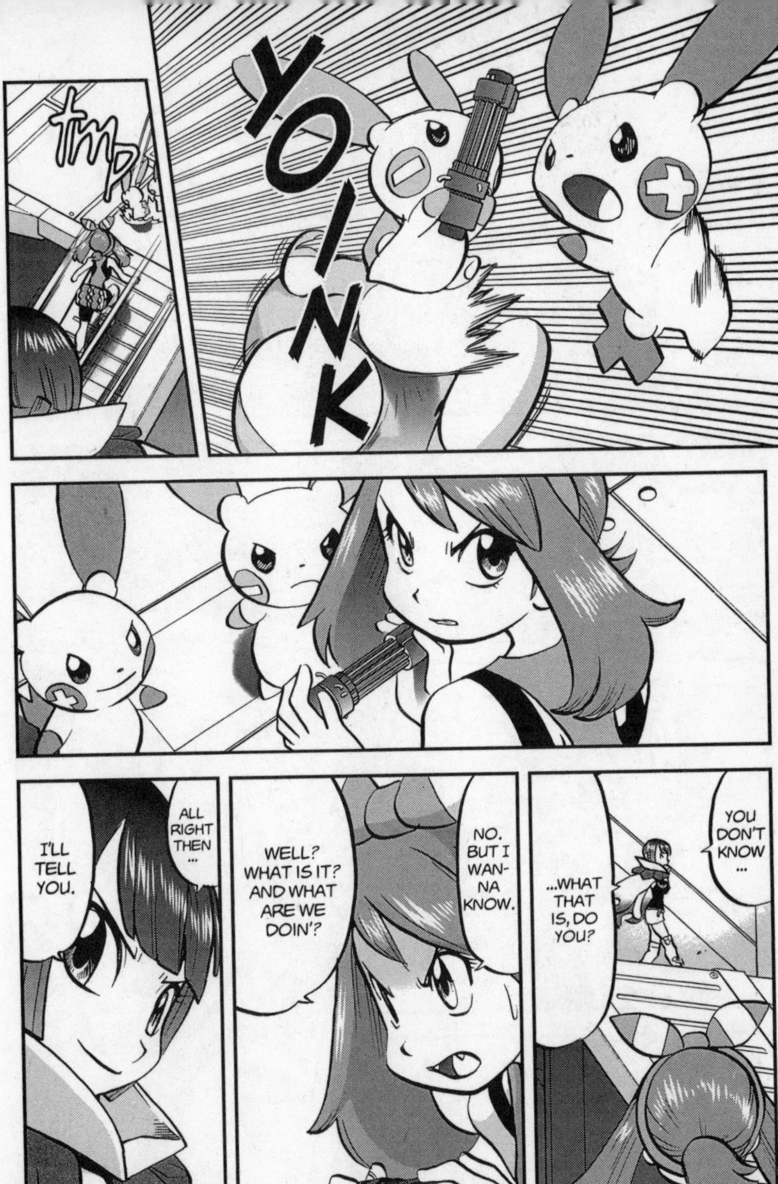
YOINK
tmp
YOU DON'T KNOW ...
...WHAT THAT IS, DO YOU?
NO. BUT I WANNA KNOW.
WELL? WHAT IS IT? AND WHAT ARE WE DOIN'?
ALL RIGHT THEN ...
I'LL TELL YOU.

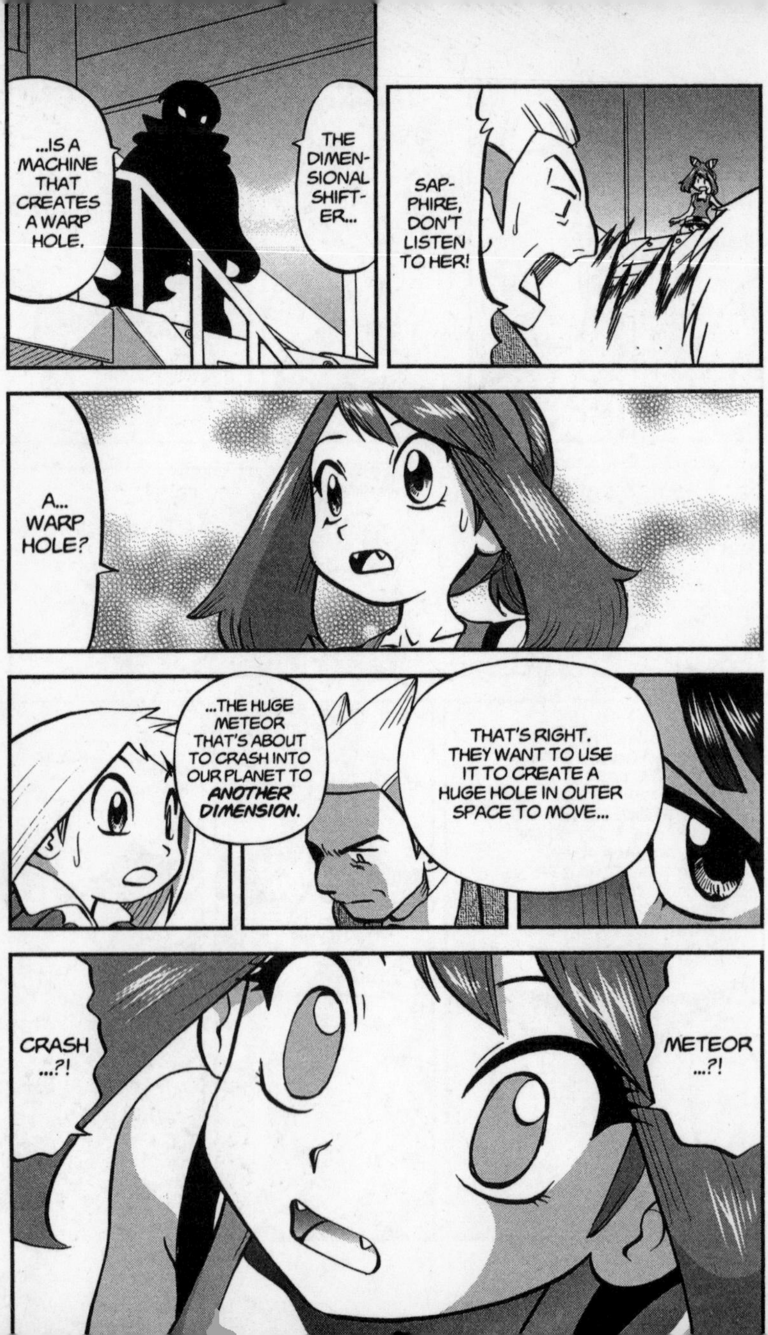
SAPPHIRE, DON'T LISTEN TO HER!
THE DIMENSIONAL SHIFTER...
...IS A MACHINE THAT CREATES A WARP HOLE.
A... WARP HOLE?
THAT'S RIGHT. THEY WANT TO USE IT TO CREATE A HUGE HOLE IN OUTER SPACE TO MOVE...
...THE HUGE METEOR THAT'S ABOUT TO CRASH INTO OUR PLANET TO ***ANOTHER DIMENSION***.
METEOR ...?!
CRASH ...?!

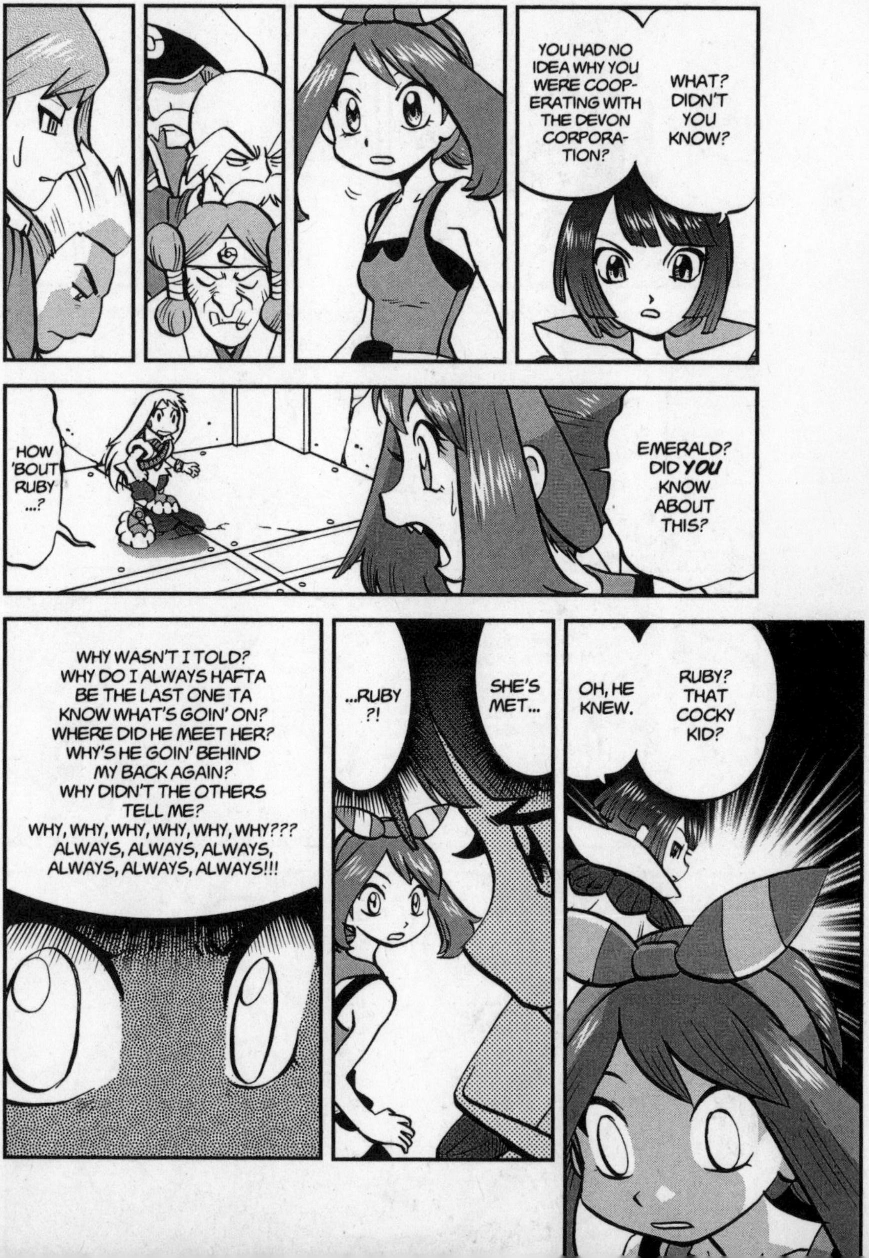
WHAT? DIDN'T YOU KNOW?
YOU HAD NO IDEA WHY YOU WERE COOP-ERATING WITH THE DEVON CORPORA-TION?
EMERALD? DID **YOU** KNOW ABOUT THIS?
HOW 'BOUT RUBY ...?
RUBY? THAT COCKY KID?
OH, HE KNEW.
SHE'S MET...
...RUBY ?!
WHY WASN'T I TOLD? WHY DO I ALWAYS HAFTA BE THE LAST ONE TA KNOW WHAT'S GOIN' ON? WHERE DID HE MEET HER? WHY'S HE GOIN' BEHIND MY BACK AGAIN? WHY DIDN'T THE OTHERS TELL ME? WHY, WHY, WHY, WHY, WHY, WHY??? ALWAYS, ALWAYS, ALWAYS, ALWAYS, ALWAYS, ALWAYS!!!

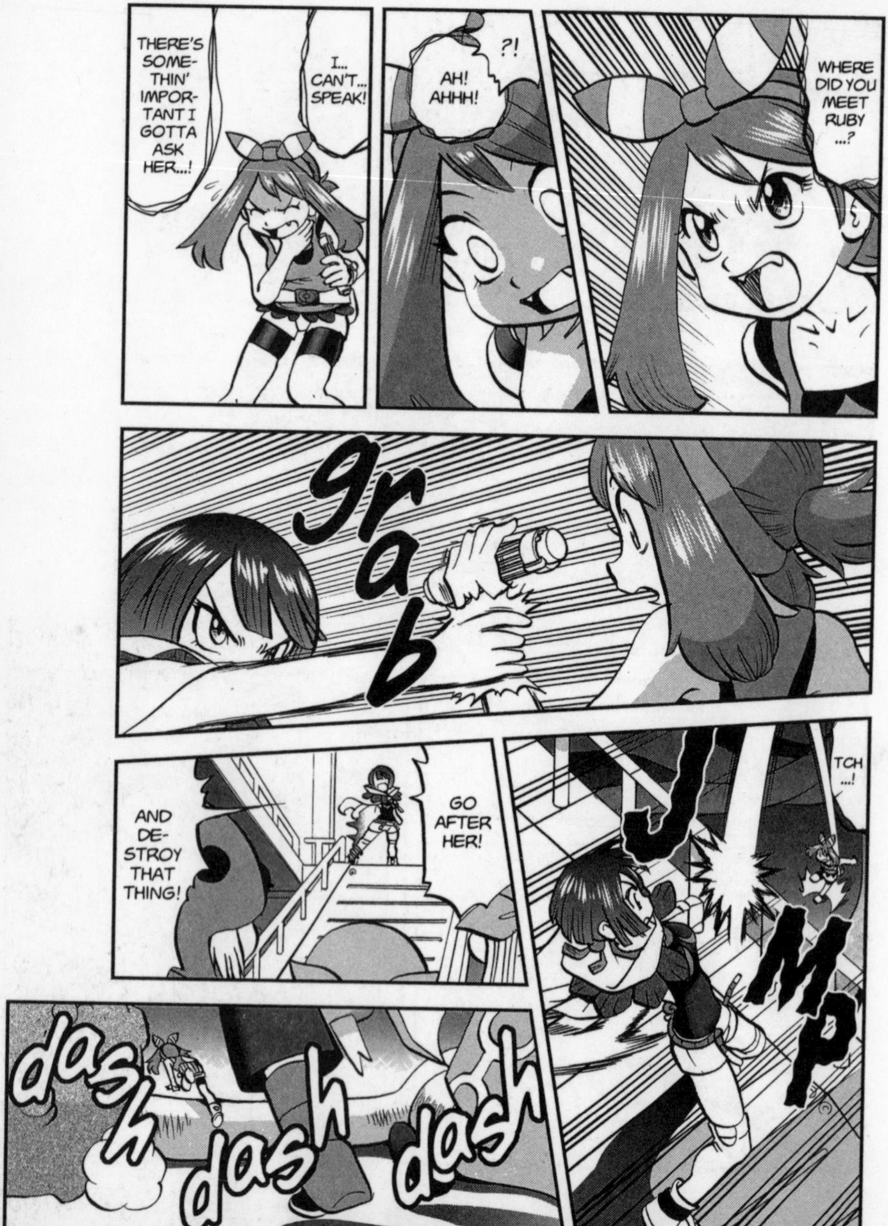
WHERE DID YOU MEET RUBY ...?
?!
AH! AHHH!
I... CAN'T... SPEAK!
THERE'S SOME-THIN' IMPOR-TANT I GOTTA ASK HER...!
grab
TCH ...!
JUMP
GO AFTER HER!
AND DE-STROY THAT THING!
dash dash dash

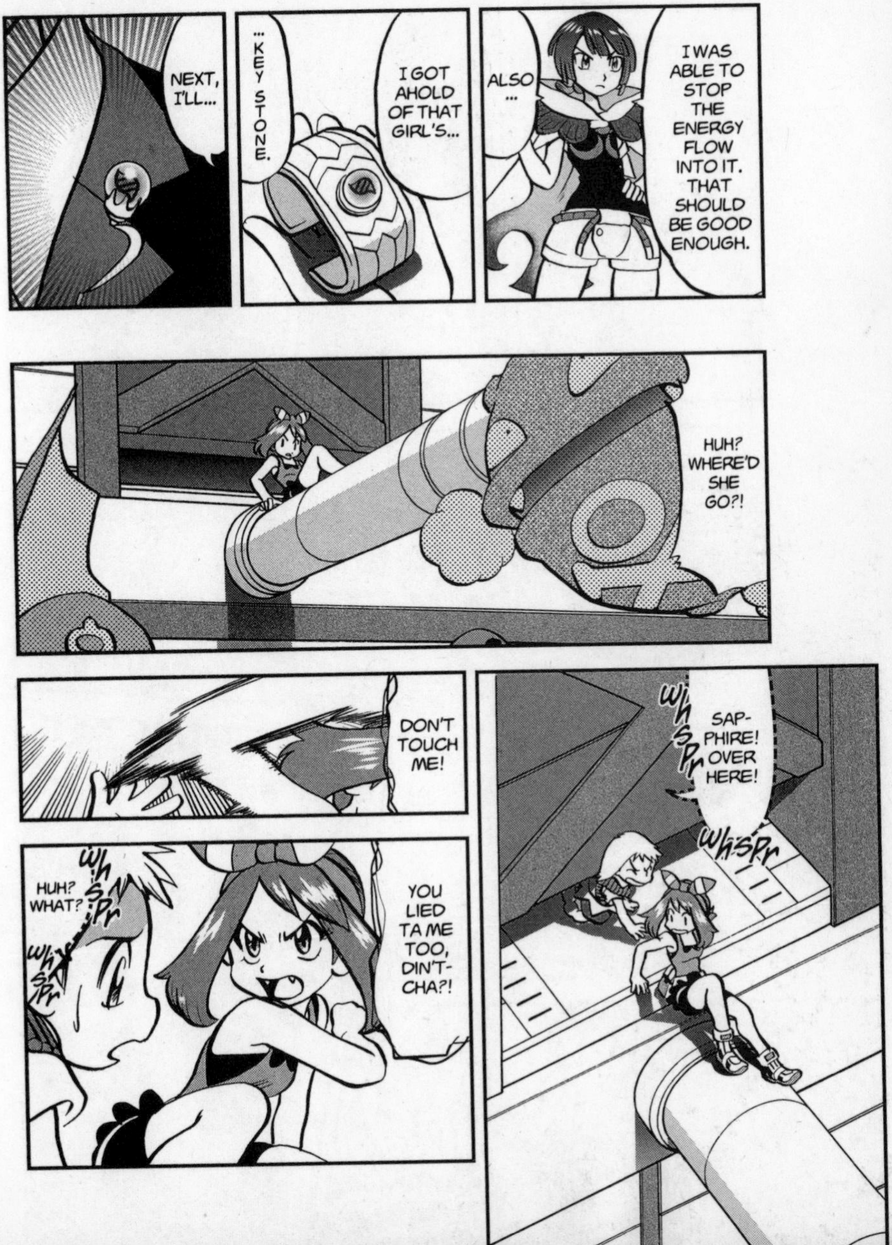
I WAS ABLE TO STOP THE ENERGY FLOW INTO IT. THAT SHOULD BE GOOD ENOUGH.
ALSO...
I GOT AHOLD OF THAT GIRL'S...
...KEY STONE.
NEXT, I'LL...
HUH? WHERE'D SHE GO?!
whspr
SAP-PHIRE! OVER HERE!
whspr
DON'T TOUCH ME!
YOU LIED TA ME TOO, DIN'T-CHA?!
HUH? WHAT?
whspr
whspr

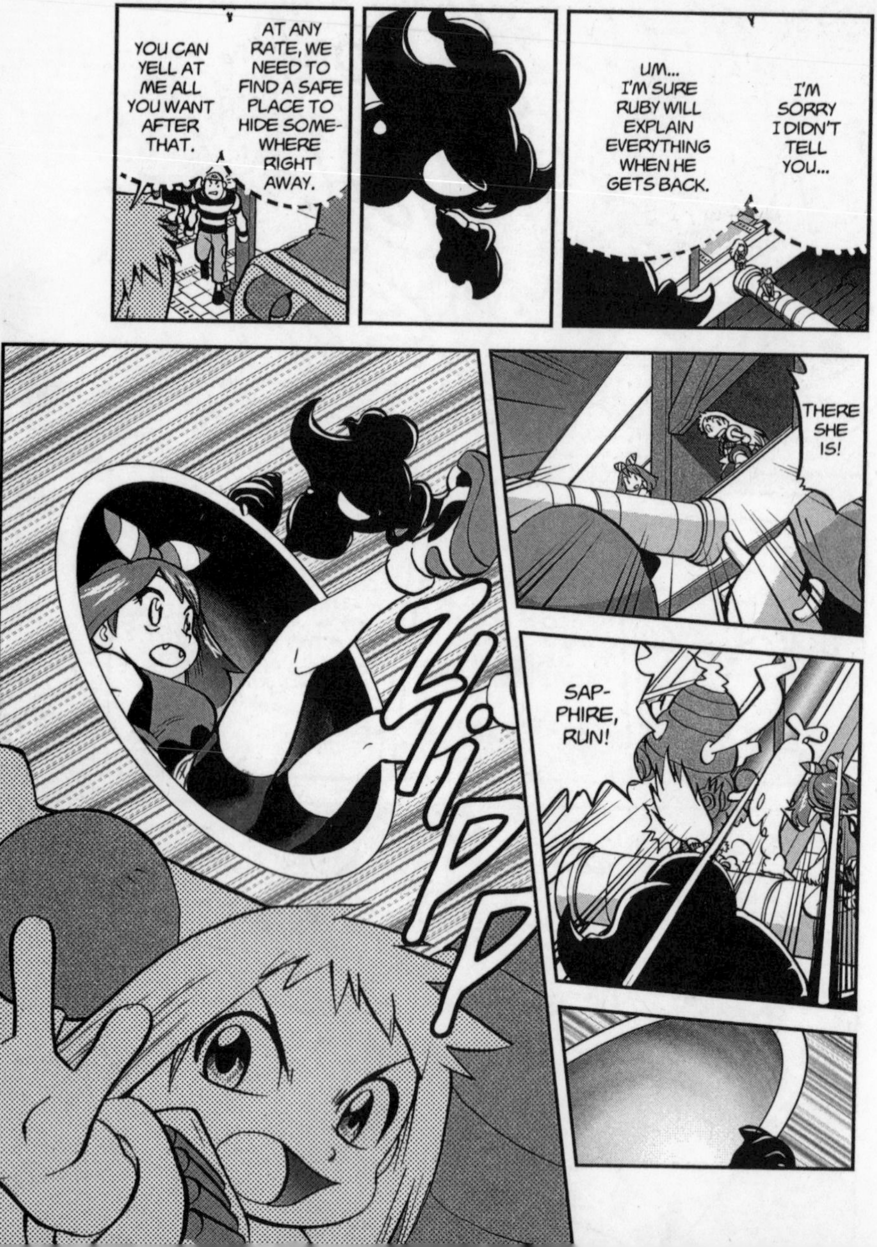
I'M SORRY I DIDN'T TELL YOU...
UM... I'M SURE RUBY WILL EXPLAIN EVERYTHING WHEN HE GETS BACK.
AT ANY RATE, WE NEED TO FIND A SAFE PLACE TO HIDE SOME-WHERE RIGHT AWAY.
YOU CAN YELL AT ME ALL YOU WANT AFTER THAT.
THERE SHE IS!
SAP-PHIRE, RUN!
ZIPP

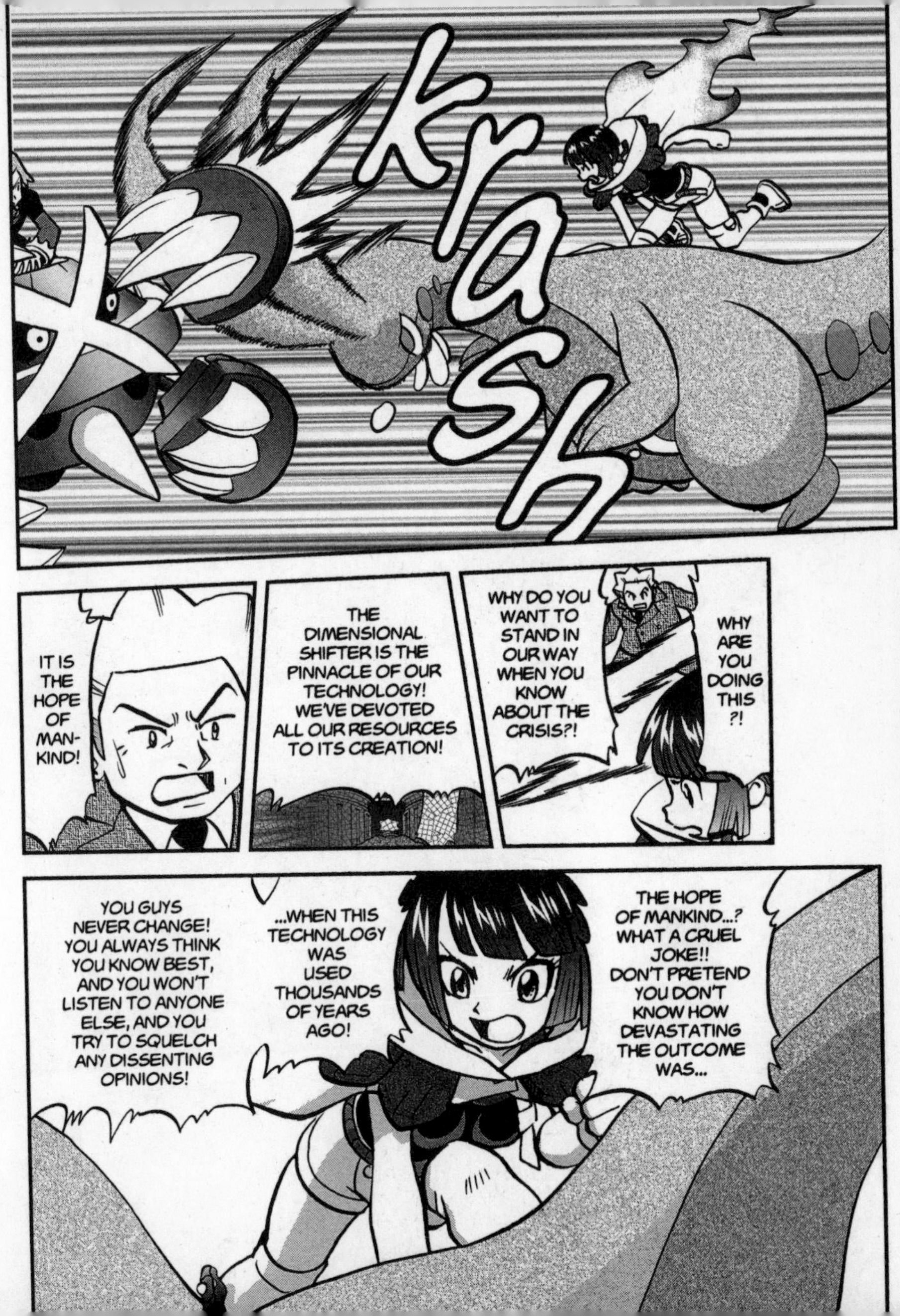
krash
WHY ARE YOU DOING THIS?!
WHY DO YOU WANT TO STAND IN OUR WAY WHEN YOU KNOW ABOUT THE CRISIS?!
THE DIMENSIONAL SHIFTER IS THE PINNACLE OF OUR TECHNOLOGY! WE'VE DEVOTED ALL OUR RESOURCES TO ITS CREATION!
IT IS THE HOPE OF MAN-KIND!
THE HOPE OF MANKIND...? WHAT A CRUEL JOKE!! DON'T PRETEND YOU DON'T KNOW HOW DEVASTATING THE OUTCOME WAS...
...WHEN THIS TECHNOLOGY WAS USED THOUSANDS OF YEARS AGO!
YOU GUYS NEVER CHANGE! YOU ALWAYS THINK YOU KNOW BEST, AND YOU WON'T LISTEN TO ANYONE ELSE, AND YOU TRY TO SQUELCH ANY DISSENTING OPINIONS!

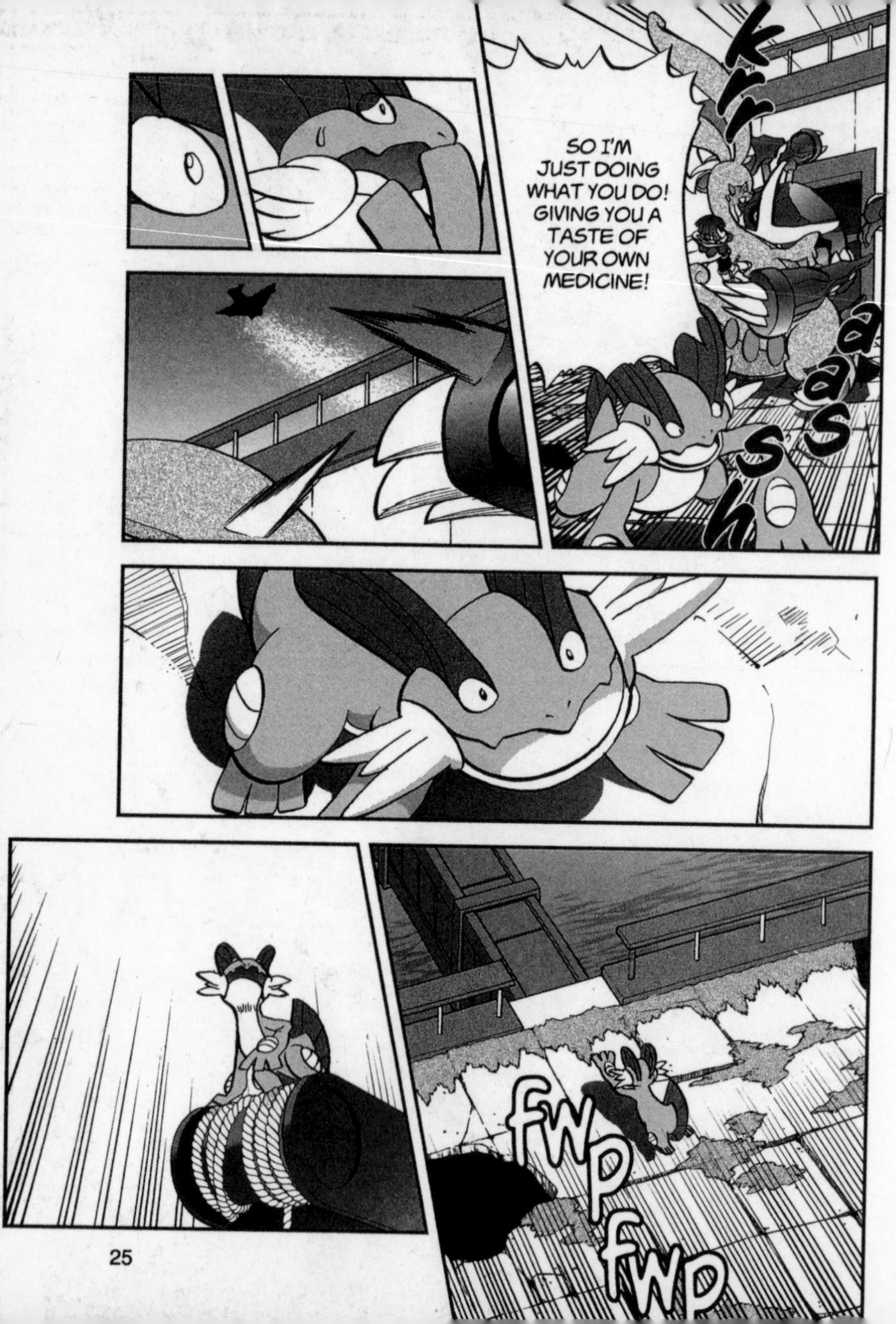
krraassh
SO I'M JUST DOING WHAT YOU DO! GIVING YOU A TASTE OF YOUR OWN MEDICINE!
fwp fwp

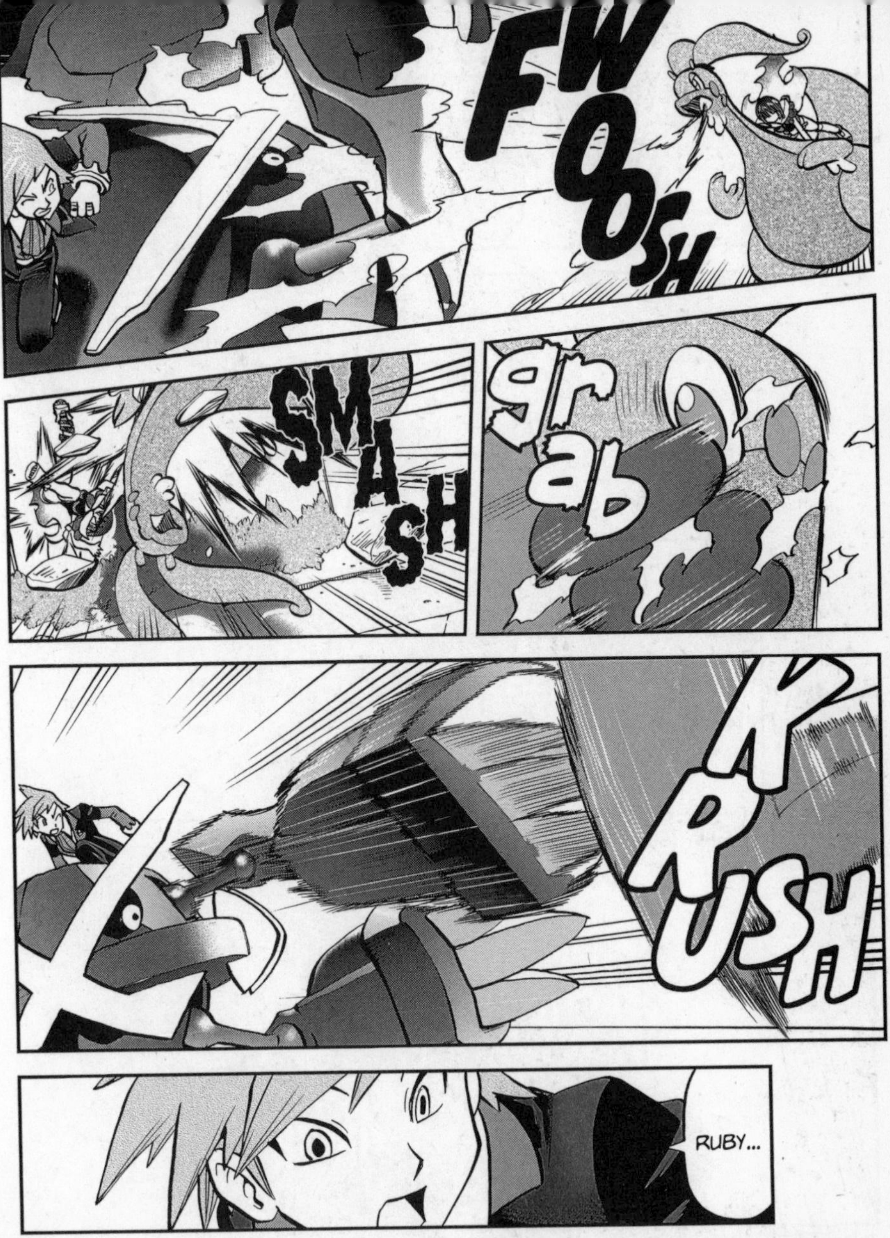
FWOOSH
grab
SMASH
KRUSH
RUBY...

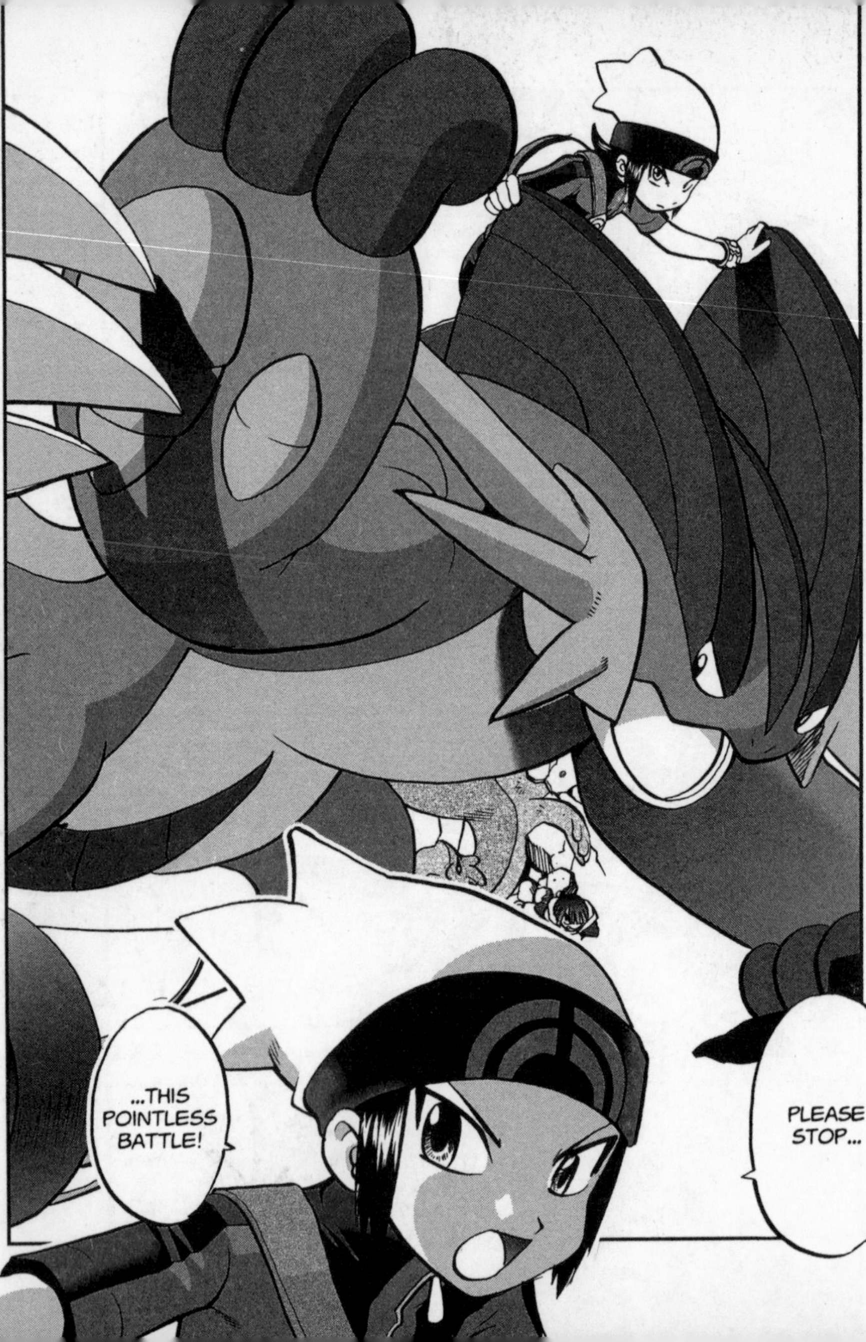
PLEASE STOP...
...THIS POINTLESS BATTLE!

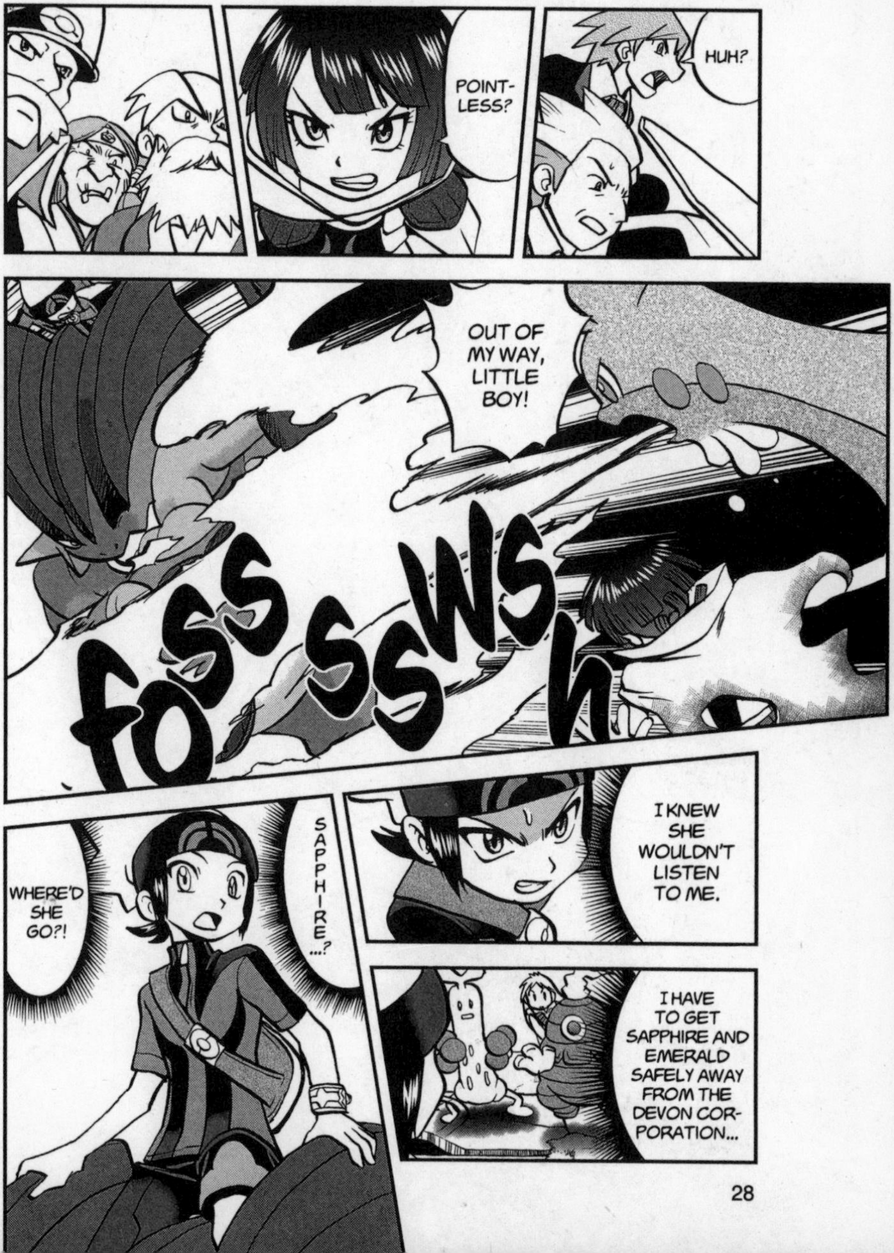
HUH?
POINT-LESS?
OUT OF MY WAY, LITTLE BOY!
fosssswsh
I KNEW SHE WOULDN'T LISTEN TO ME.
I HAVE TO GET SAPPHIRE AND EMERALD SAFELY AWAY FROM THE DEVON COR-PORATION...
SAPPHIRE...?
WHERE'D SHE GO?!

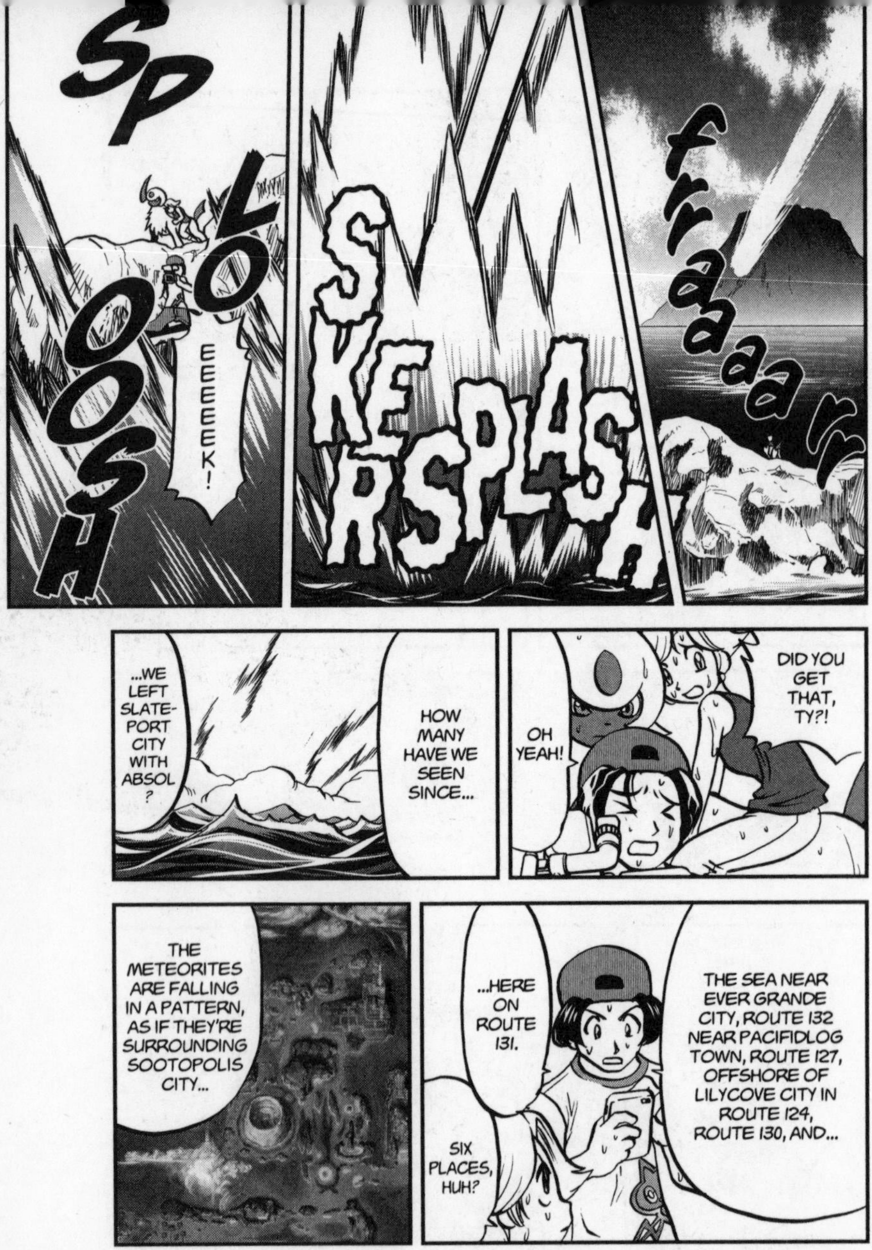
fraaaarm
SKERSPLASH
SPLOOOSH
EEEEEEK!
DID YOU GET THAT, TY?!
OH YEAH!
HOW MANY HAVE WE SEEN SINCE...
...WE LEFT SLATE-PORT CITY WITH ABSOL?
THE SEA NEAR EVER GRANDE CITY, ROUTE 132 NEAR PACIFIDLOG TOWN, ROUTE 127, OFFSHORE OF LILYCOVE CITY IN ROUTE 124, ROUTE 130, AND...
...HERE ON ROUTE 131.
SIX PLACES, HUH?
THE METEORITES ARE FALLING IN A PATTERN, AS IF THEY'RE SURROUNDING SOOTOPOLIS CITY...

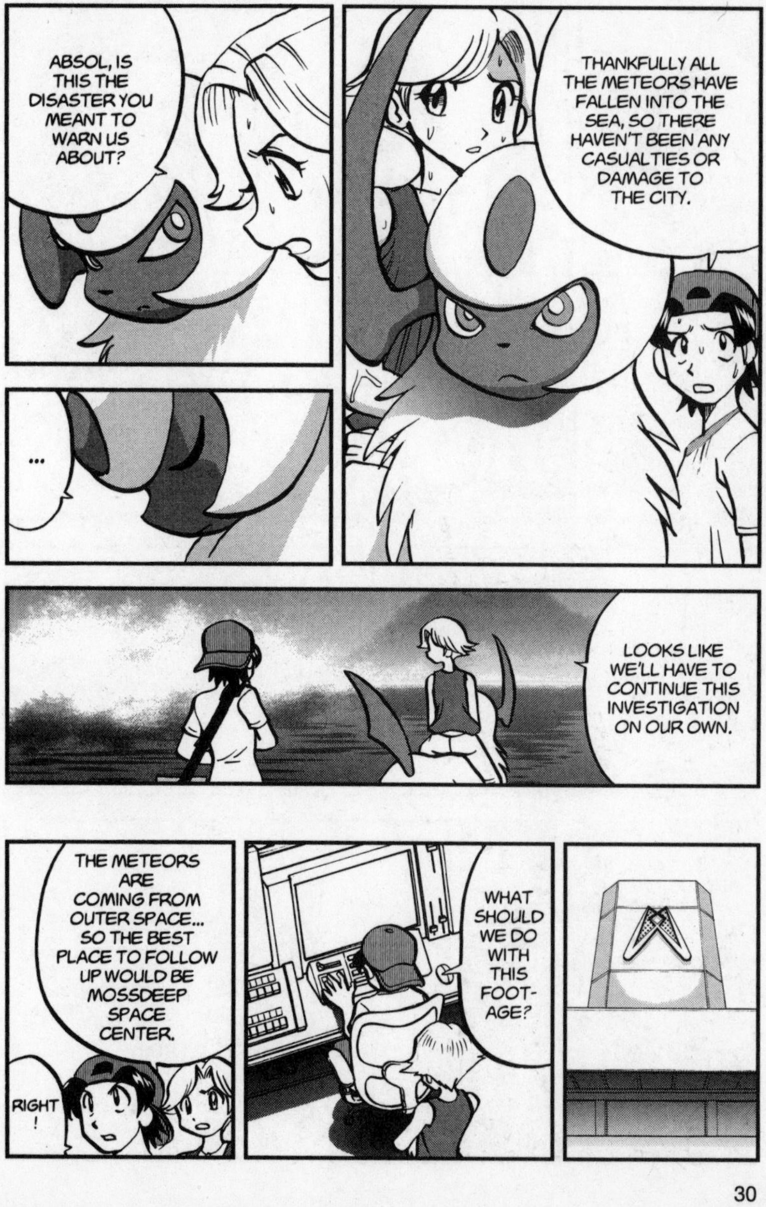
THANKFULLY ALL THE METEORS HAVE FALLEN INTO THE SEA, SO THERE HAVEN'T BEEN ANY CASUALTIES OR DAMAGE TO THE CITY.
ABSOL, IS THIS THE DISASTER YOU MEANT TO WARN US ABOUT?
...
LOOKS LIKE WE'LL HAVE TO CONTINUE THIS INVESTIGATION ON OUR OWN.
WHAT SHOULD WE DO WITH THIS FOOT-AGE?
THE METEORS ARE COMING FROM OUTER SPACE... SO THE BEST PLACE TO FOLLOW UP WOULD BE MOSSDEEP SPACE CENTER.
RIGHT!

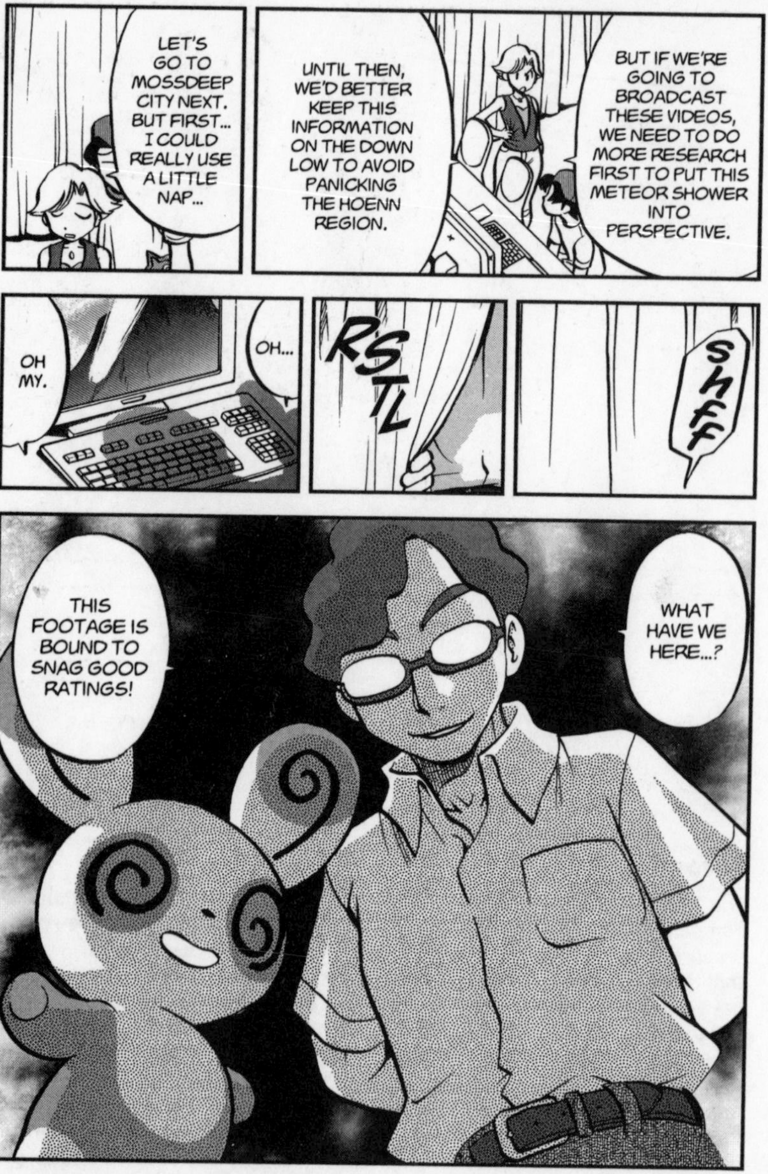
BUT IF WE'RE GOING TO BROADCAST THESE VIDEOS, WE NEED TO DO MORE RESEARCH FIRST TO PUT THIS METEOR SHOWER INTO PERSPECTIVE.
UNTIL THEN, WE'D BETTER KEEP THIS INFORMATION ON THE DOWN LOW TO AVOID PANICKING THE HOENN REGION.
LET'S GO TO MOSSDEEP CITY NEXT. BUT FIRST... I COULD REALLY USE A LITTLE NAP...
SNFF
RSTL
OH...
OH MY.
WHAT HAVE WE HERE...?
THIS FOOTAGE IS BOUND TO SNAG GOOD RATINGS!

GREATER MAUVILLE HOLDINGS

The Devon Corporation's rival
company that excavated natural
resources at Sea Mauville. It is said
that there was fierce competition
between the two companies.
But the company's New Mauville
Project came to a standstill, which
eventually led to the closure of Sea
Mauville. Many of the workers were
reemployed at the building dock in
Slateport.

SEA MAUVILLE

A mine once owned by Greater
Mauville Holdings to excavate
ocean floor resources. It
was closed down several
decades ago. The facility was
scheduled to be torn apart
immediately, but the result
of an environmental survey
discovered that a unique habitat
had been created and it is now
kept as a natural reserve.

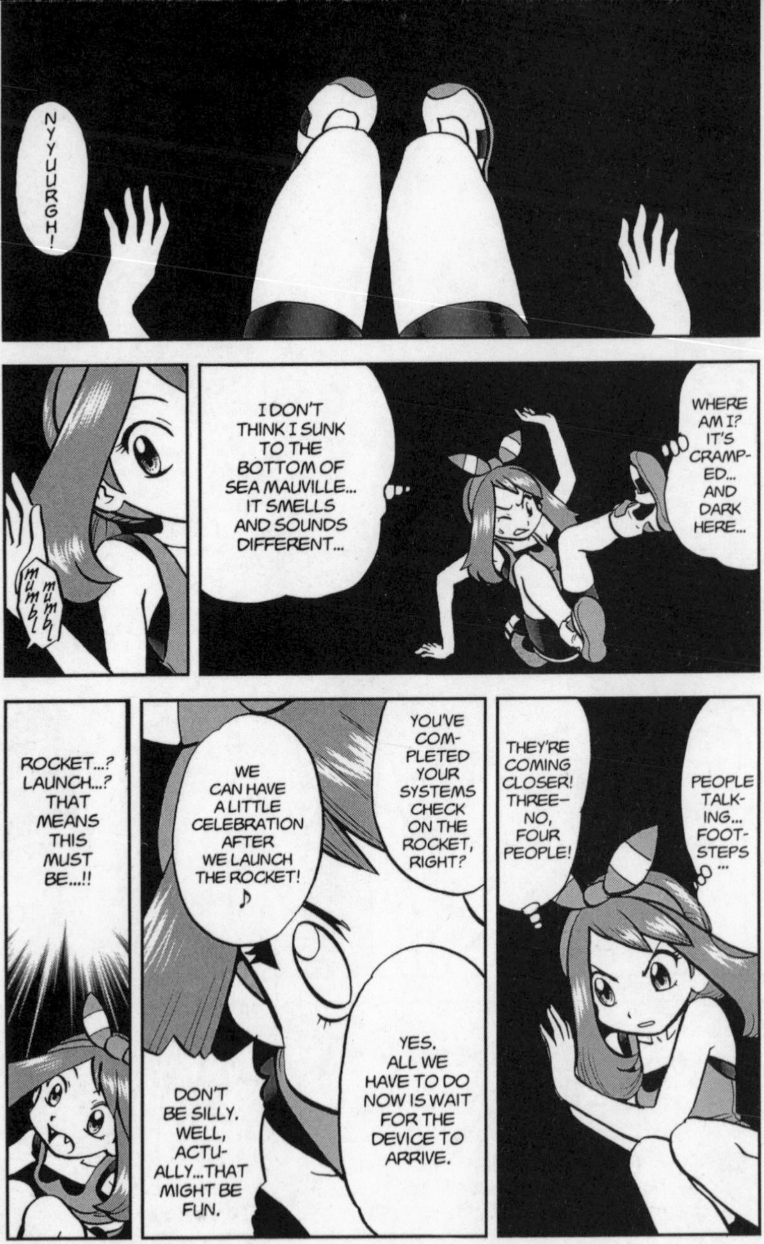
NYYUURGH!
WHERE AM I? IT'S CRAMPED... AND DARK HERE...
I DON'T THINK I SUNK TO THE BOTTOM OF SEA MAUVILLE... IT SMELLS AND SOUNDS DIFFERENT...
mumbl mumbl
PEOPLE TALKING... FOOTSTEPS...
THEY'RE COMING CLOSER! THREE— NO, FOUR PEOPLE!
YOU'VE COMPLETED YOUR SYSTEMS CHECK ON THE ROCKET, RIGHT?
WE CAN HAVE A LITTLE CELEBRATION AFTER WE LAUNCH THE ROCKET! ♪
YES. ALL WE HAVE TO DO NOW IS WAIT FOR THE DEVICE TO ARRIVE.
DON'T BE SILLY. WELL, ACTUALLY...THAT MIGHT BE FUN.
ROCKET...? LAUNCH...? THAT MEANS THIS MUST BE...!!

Omega Alpha Adventure 9

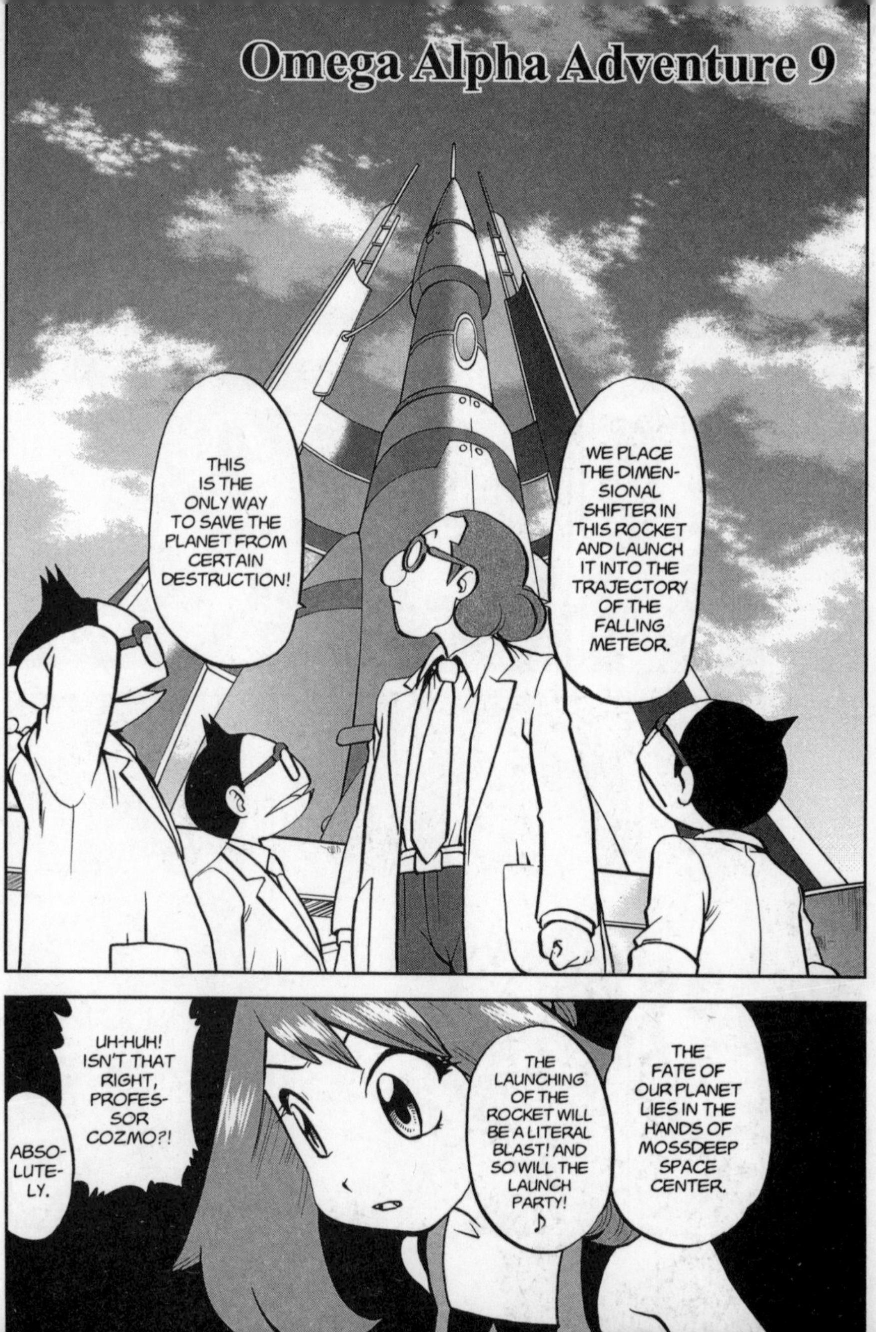
WE PLACE THE DIMEN-SIONAL SHIFTER IN THIS ROCKET AND LAUNCH IT INTO THE TRAJECTORY OF THE FALLING METEOR.
THIS IS THE ONLY WAY TO SAVE THE PLANET FROM CERTAIN DESTRUCTION!
THE FATE OF OUR PLANET LIES IN THE HANDS OF MOSSDEEP SPACE CENTER.
THE LAUNCHING OF THE ROCKET WILL BE A LITERAL BLAST! AND SO WILL THE LAUNCH PARTY! ♪
UH-HUH! ISN'T THAT RIGHT, PROFES-SOR COZMO?!
ABSO-LUTE-LY.

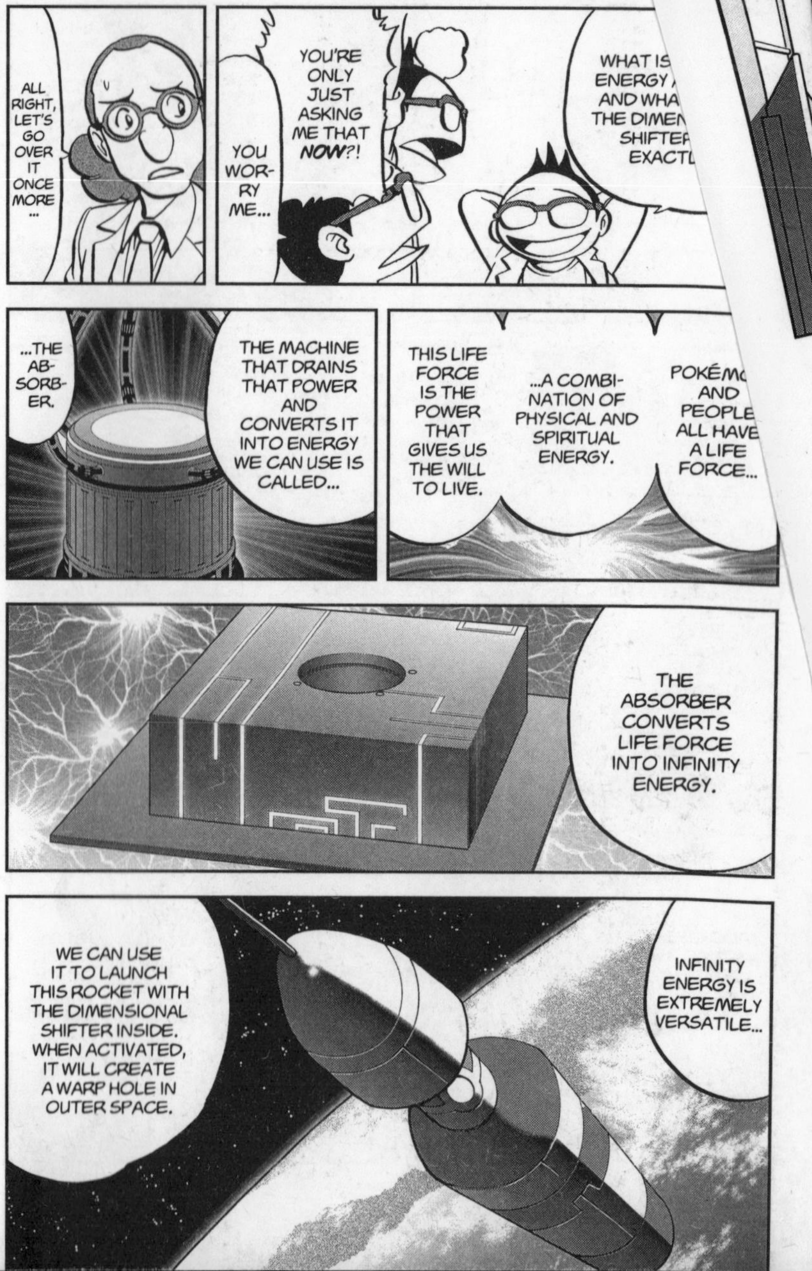
WHAT IS ENERGY AND WHA THE DIMEN SHIFTER EXACTL
YOU'RE ONLY JUST ASKING ME THAT NOW?!
YOU WORRY ME...
ALL RIGHT, LET'S GO OVER IT ONCE MORE...
POKÉMO AND PEOPLE ALL HAVE A LIFE FORCE...
...A COMBINATION OF PHYSICAL AND SPIRITUAL ENERGY.
THIS LIFE FORCE IS THE POWER THAT GIVES US THE WILL TO LIVE.
THE MACHINE THAT DRAINS THAT POWER AND CONVERTS IT INTO ENERGY WE CAN USE IS CALLED...
...THE ABSORBER.
THE ABSORBER CONVERTS LIFE FORCE INTO INFINITY ENERGY.
INFINITY ENERGY IS EXTREMELY VERSATILE...
WE CAN USE IT TO LAUNCH THIS ROCKET WITH THE DIMENSIONAL SHIFTER INSIDE. WHEN ACTIVATED, IT WILL CREATE A WARP HOLE IN OUTER SPACE.
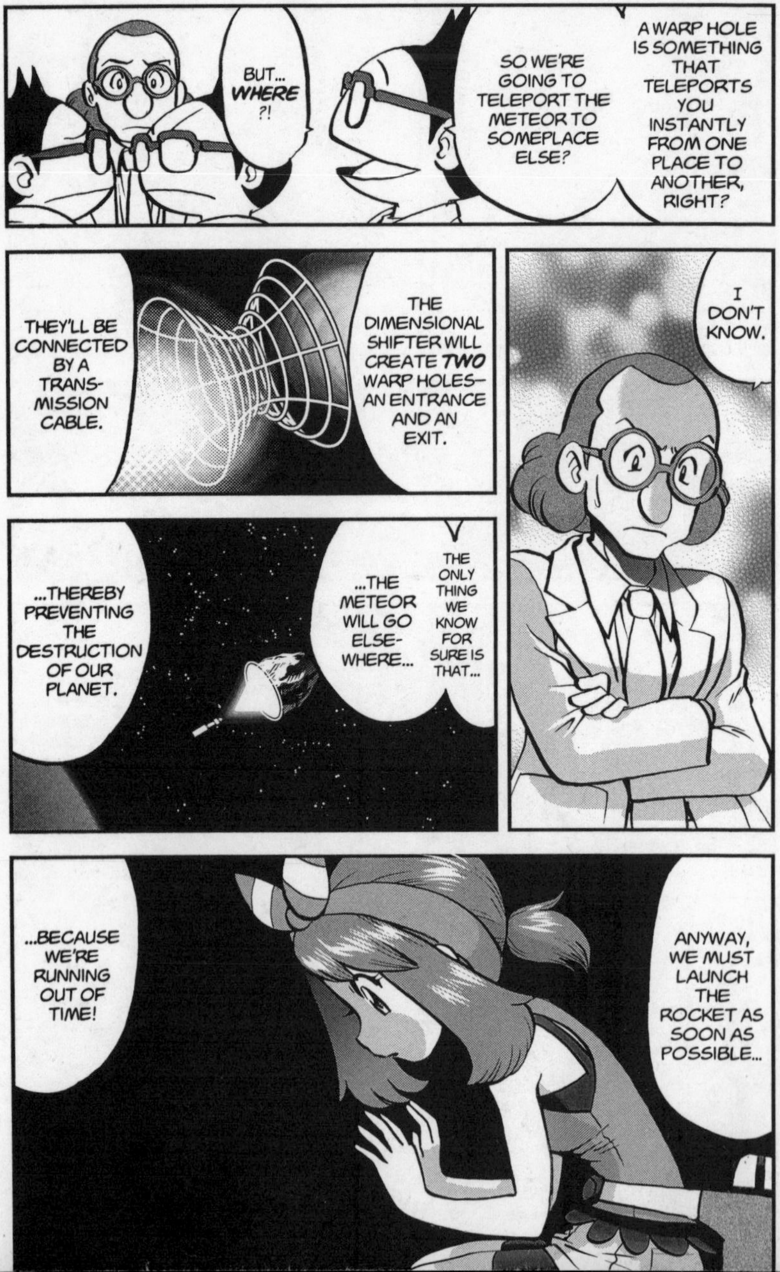
A WARP HOLE IS SOMETHING THAT TELEPORTS YOU INSTANTLY FROM ONE PLACE TO ANOTHER, RIGHT?
SO WE'RE GOING TO TELEPORT THE METEOR TO SOMEPLACE ELSE?
BUT... WHERE?!
I DON'T KNOW.
THE DIMENSIONAL SHIFTER WILL CREATE TWO WARP HOLES—AN ENTRANCE AND AN EXIT.
THEY'LL BE CONNECTED BY A TRANSMISSION CABLE.
THE ONLY THING WE KNOW FOR SURE IS THAT...
...THE METEOR WILL GO ELSEWHERE...
...THEREBY PREVENTING THE DESTRUCTION OF OUR PLANET.
ANYWAY, WE MUST LAUNCH THE ROCKET AS SOON AS POSSIBLE...
...BECAUSE WE'RE RUNNING OUT OF TIME!

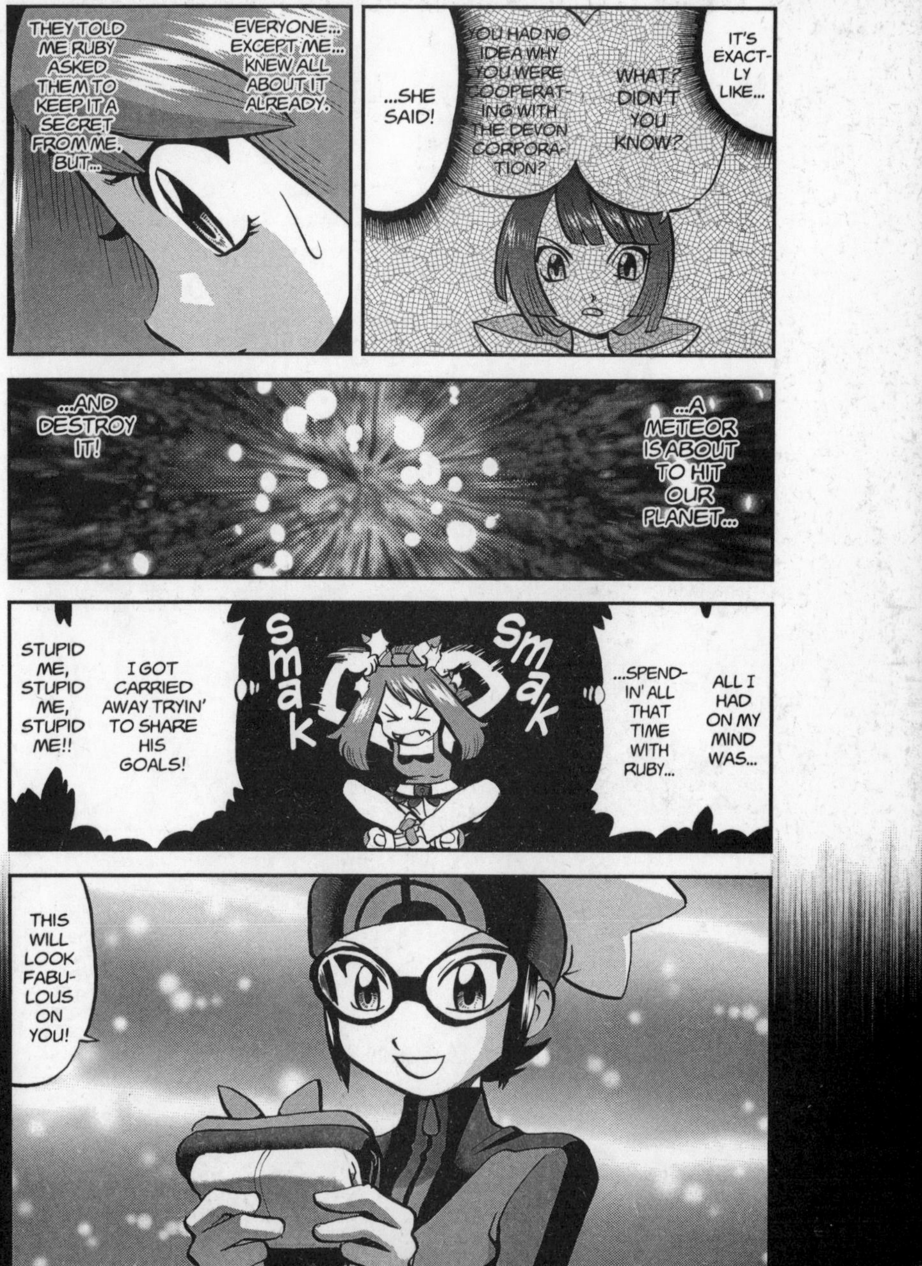
IT'S EXACTLY LIKE...
WHAT? DIDN'T YOU KNOW?
YOU HAD NO IDEA WHY YOU WERE COOPERATING WITH THE DEVON CORPORATION?
...SHE SAID!
EVERYONE... EXCEPT ME... KNEW ALL ABOUT IT ALREADY.
THEY TOLD ME RUBY ASKED THEM TO KEEP IT A SECRET FROM ME. BUT...
...A METEOR IS ABOUT TO HIT OUR PLANET...
...AND DESTROY IT!
ALL I HAD ON MY MIND WAS...
...SPENDIN' ALL THAT TIME WITH RUBY...
SMAK
SMAK
I GOT CARRIED AWAY TRYIN' TO SHARE HIS GOALS!
STUPID ME, STUPID ME, STUPID ME!!
THIS WILL LOOK FABULOUS ON YOU!

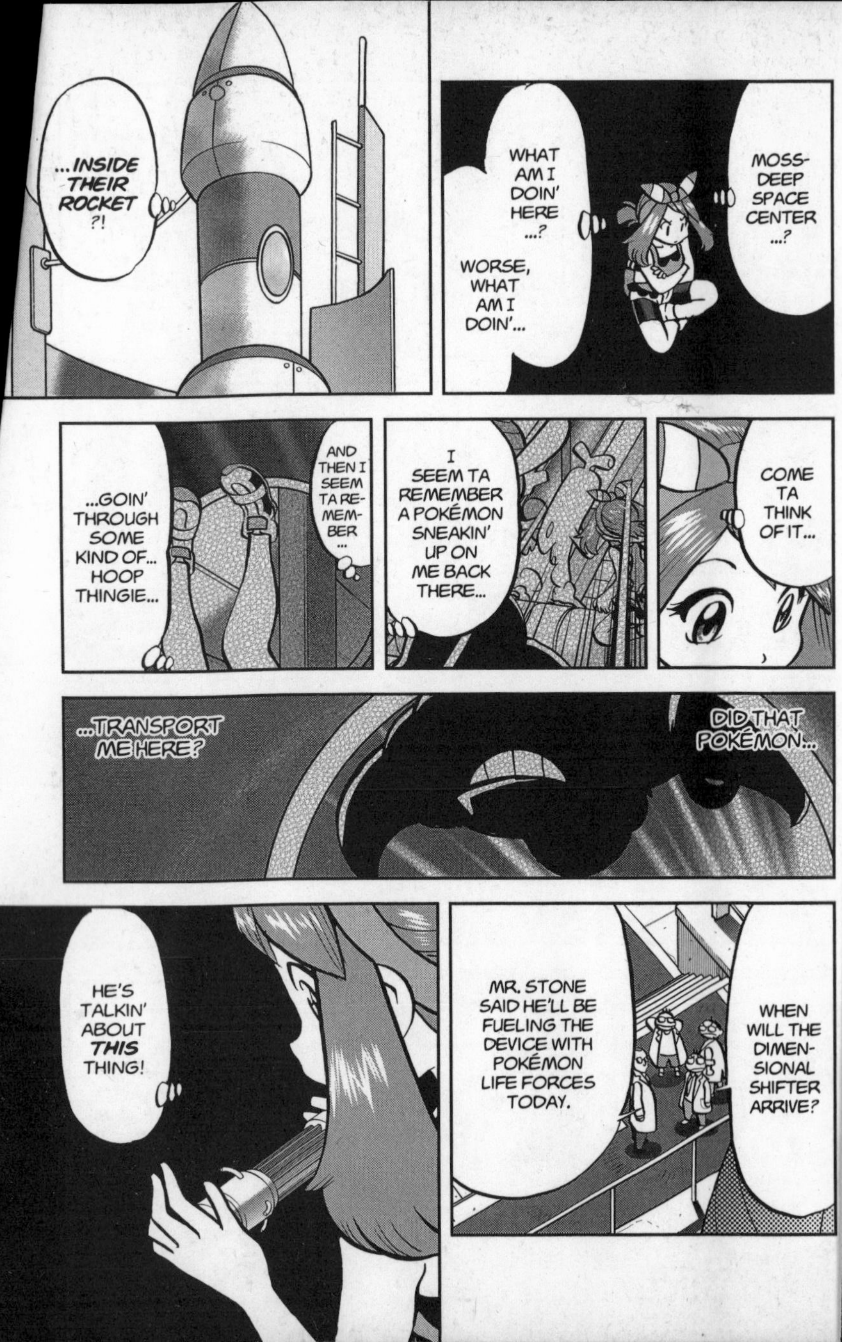
MOSS-DEEP SPACE CENTER ...?
WHAT AM I DOIN' HERE ...?
WORSE, WHAT AM I DOIN'...
...INSIDE THEIR ROCKET ?!
COME TA THINK OF IT...
I SEEM TA REMEMBER A POKÉMON SNEAKIN' UP ON ME BACK THERE...
AND THEN I SEEM TA REMEMBER ...
...GOIN' THROUGH SOME KIND OF... HOOP THINGIE...
DID THAT POKÉMON...
...TRANSPORT ME HERE?
WHEN WILL THE DIMENSIONAL SHIFTER ARRIVE?
MR. STONE SAID HE'LL BE FUELING THE DEVICE WITH POKÉMON LIFE FORCES TODAY.
HE'S TALKIN' ABOUT THIS THING!

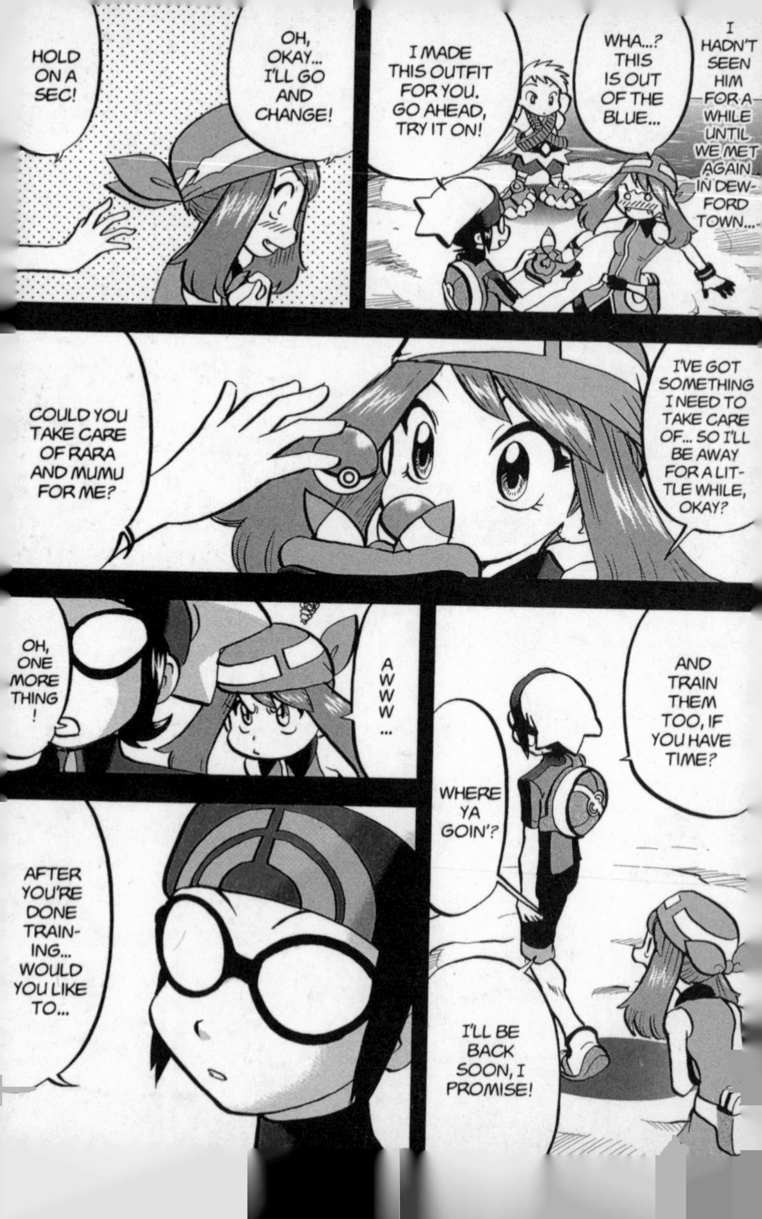
I HADN'T SEEN HIM FOR A WHILE UNTIL WE MET AGAIN IN DEWFORD TOWN...
WHA...? THIS IS OUT OF THE BLUE...
I MADE THIS OUTFIT FOR YOU. GO AHEAD, TRY IT ON!
OH, OKAY... I'LL GO AND CHANGE!
HOLD ON A SEC!
I'VE GOT SOMETHING I NEED TO TAKE CARE OF... SO I'LL BE AWAY FOR A LITTLE WHILE, OKAY?
COULD YOU TAKE CARE OF RARA AND MUMU FOR ME?
AND TRAIN THEM TOO, IF YOU HAVE TIME?
WHERE YA GOIN'?
I'LL BE BACK SOON, I PROMISE!
AWWW...
OH, ONE MORE THING!
AFTER YOU'RE DONE TRAINING... WOULD YOU LIKE TO...

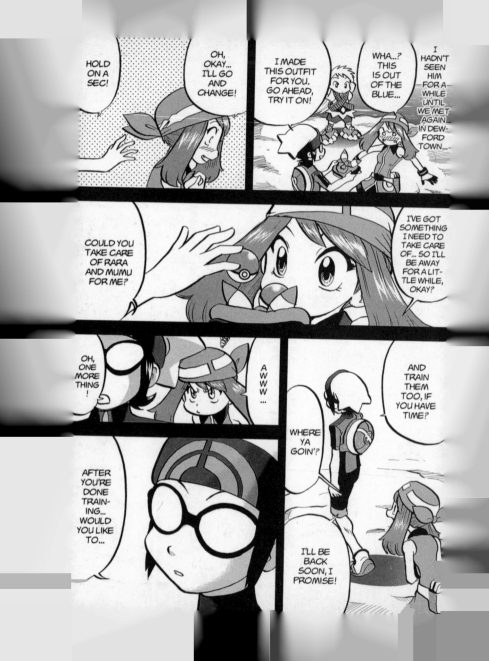

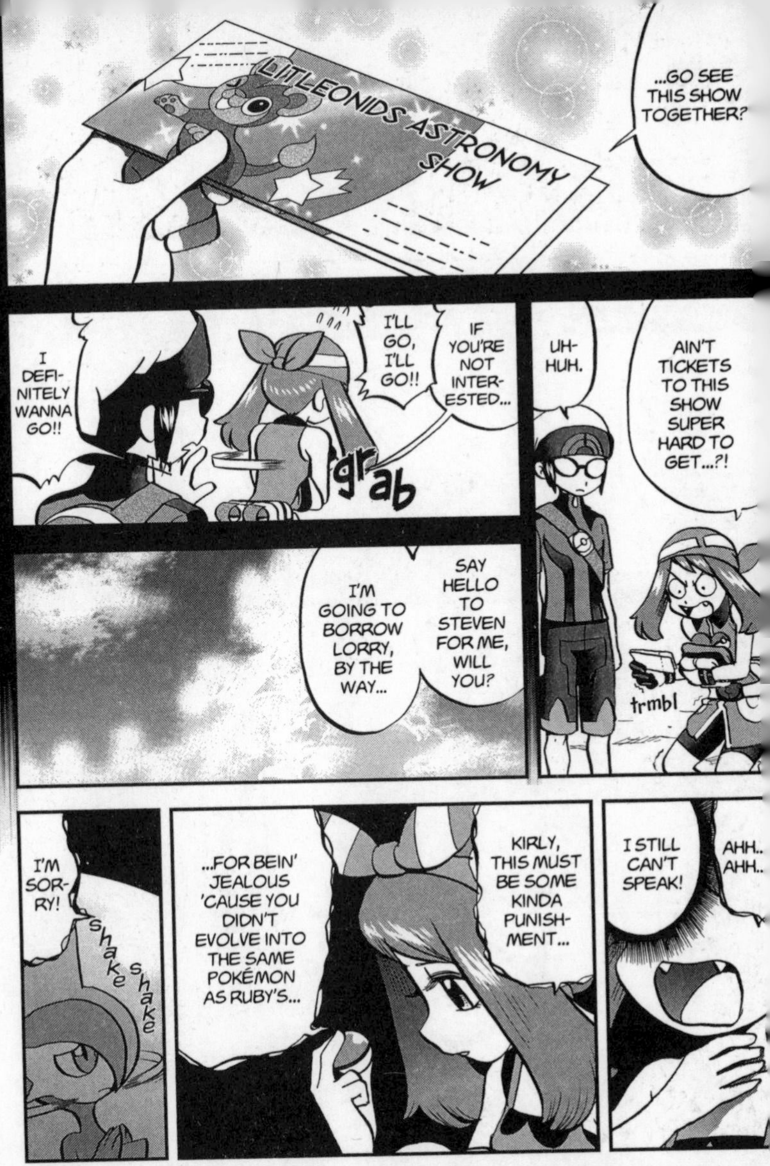
...GO SEE THIS SHOW TOGETHER?
LITLEONIDS ASTRONOMY SHOW
AIN'T TICKETS TO THIS SHOW SUPER HARD TO GET...?!
UH-HUH.
trmbl
IF YOU'RE NOT INTERESTED...
I'LL GO, I'LL GO!!
I DEFINITELY WANNA GO!!
grab
SAY HELLO TO STEVEN FOR ME, WILL YOU?
I'M GOING TO BORROW LORRY, BY THE WAY...
AHH.. AHH..
I STILL CAN'T SPEAK!
KIRLY, THIS MUST BE SOME KINDA PUNISHMENT...
...FOR BEIN' JEALOUS 'CAUSE YOU DIDN'T EVOLVE INTO THE SAME POKÉMON AS RUBY'S...
I'M SORRY!
shake shake

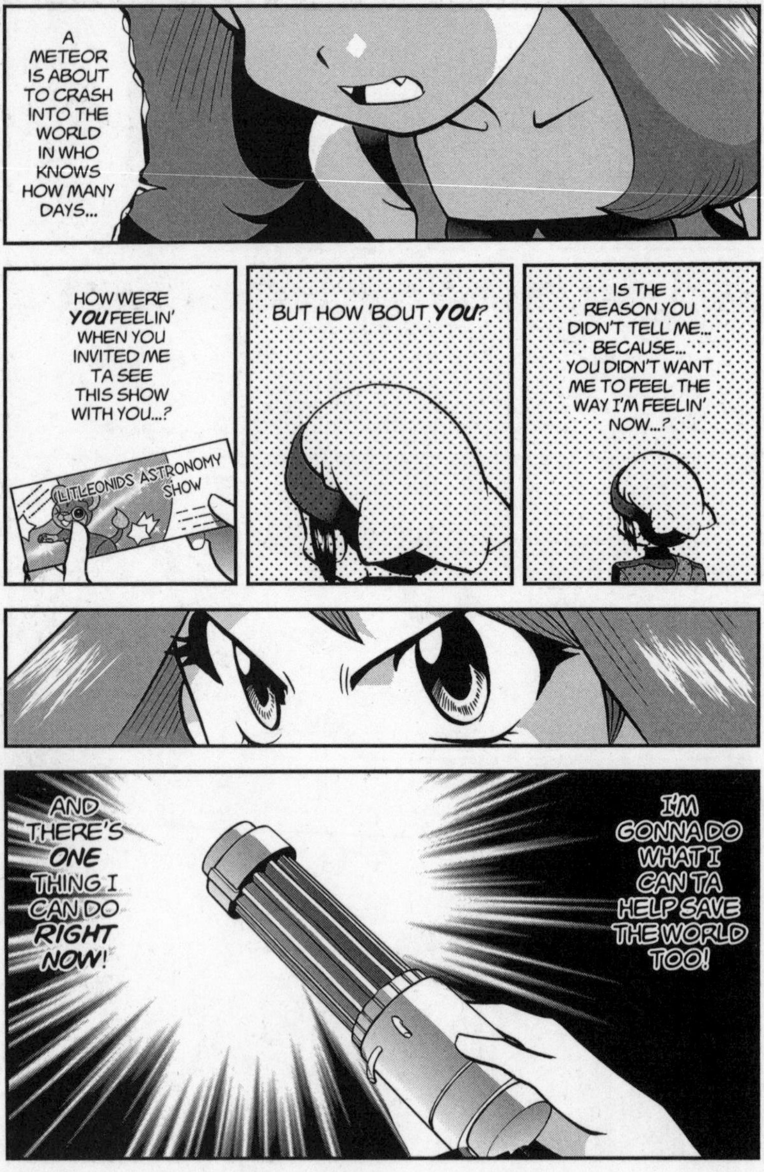
A METEOR IS ABOUT TO CRASH INTO THE WORLD IN WHO KNOWS HOW MANY DAYS...
IS THE REASON YOU DIDN'T TELL ME... BECAUSE... YOU DIDN'T WANT ME TO FEEL THE WAY I'M FEELIN' NOW...?
BUT HOW 'BOUT YOU?
HOW WERE YOU FEELIN' WHEN YOU INVITED ME TA SEE THIS SHOW WITH YOU...?
LITLEONIDS ASTRONOMY SHOW
AND THERE'S ONE THING I CAN DO RIGHT NOW!
I'M GONNA DO WHAT I CAN TA HELP SAVE THE WORLD TOO!

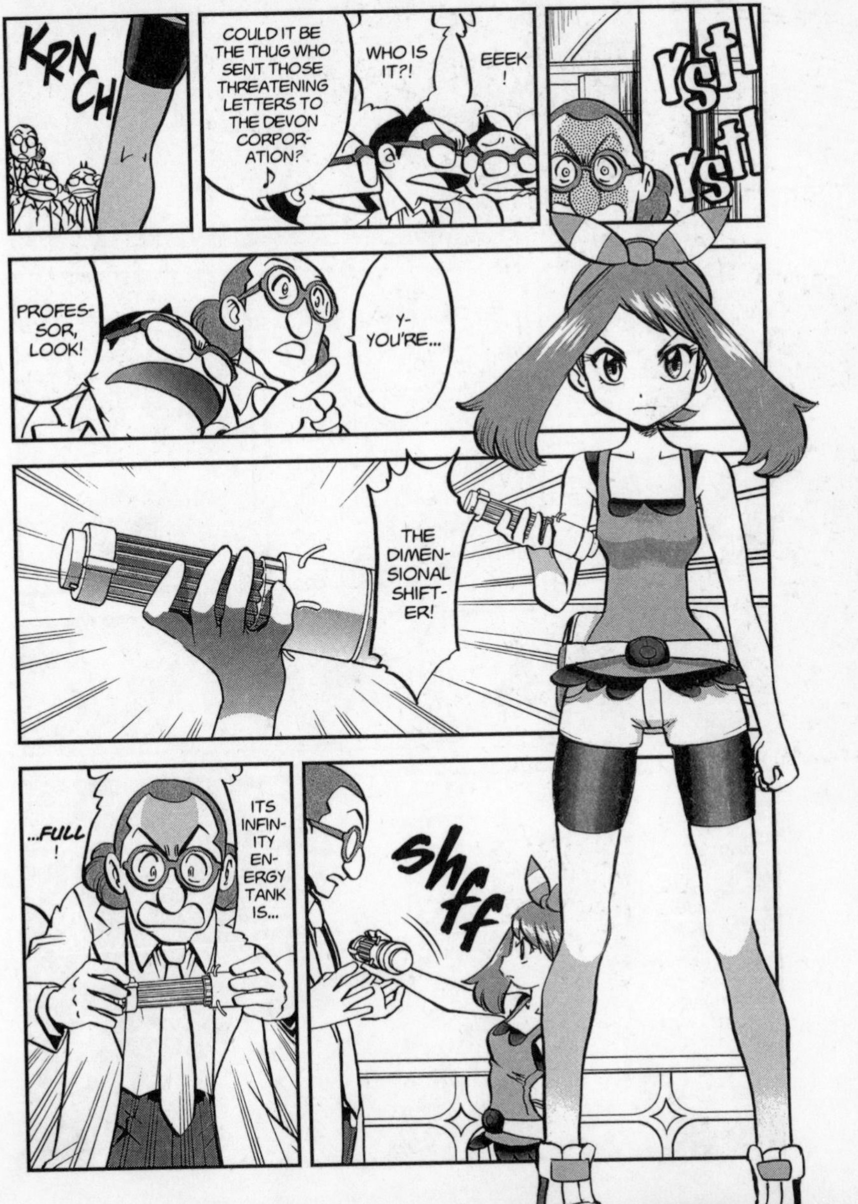
rstl
rstl
EEEK!
WHO IS IT?!
COULD IT BE THE THUG WHO SENT THOSE THREATENING LETTERS TO THE DEVON CORPORATION? ♪
KRNCH
Y-YOU'RE...
PROFESSOR, LOOK!
THE DIMENSIONAL SHIFTER!
shff
ITS INFINITY ENERGY TANK IS...
...FULL!

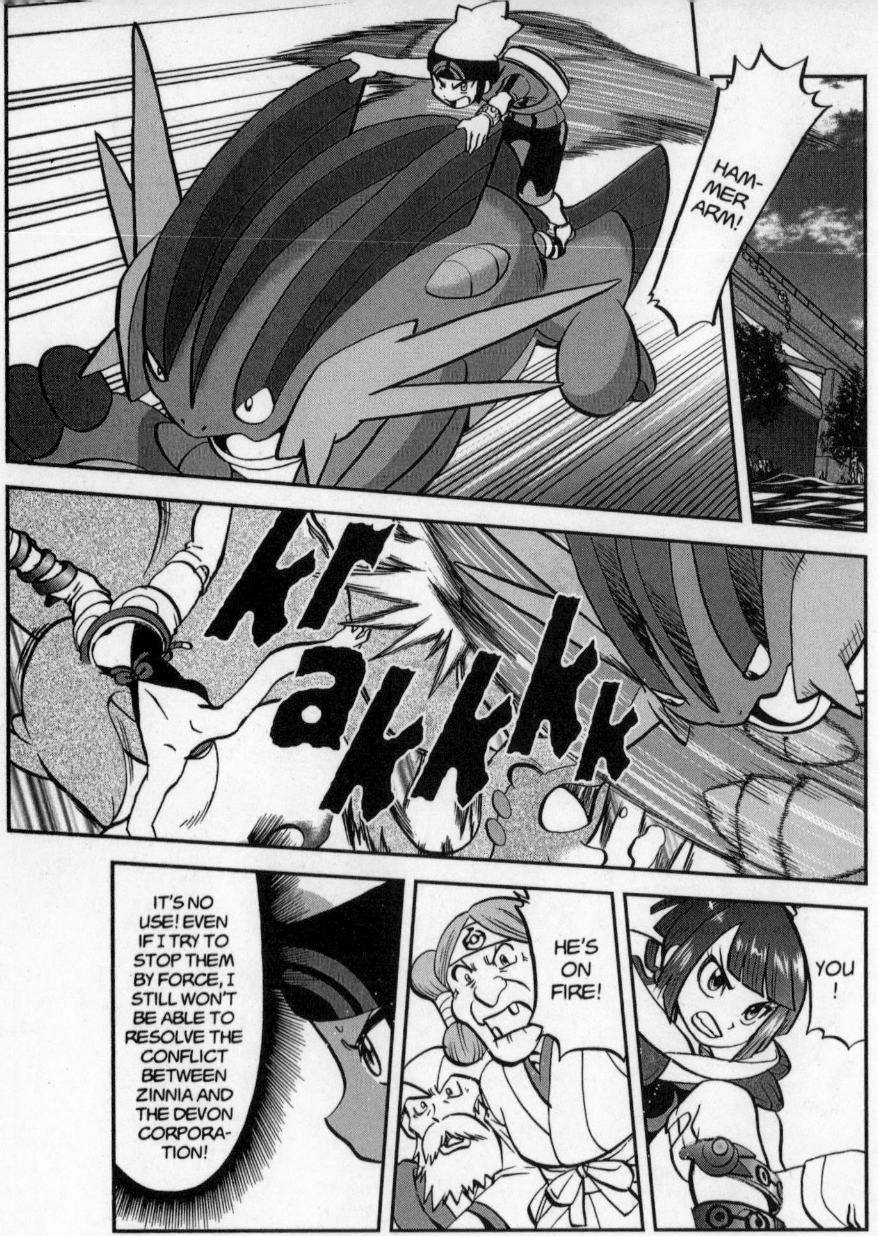
HAM-MER ARM!
KRAKKKK
YOU!
HE'S ON FIRE!
IT'S NO USE! EVEN IF I TRY TO STOP THEM BY FORCE, I STILL WON'T BE ABLE TO RESOLVE THE CONFLICT BETWEEN ZINNIA AND THE DEVON CORPORATION!

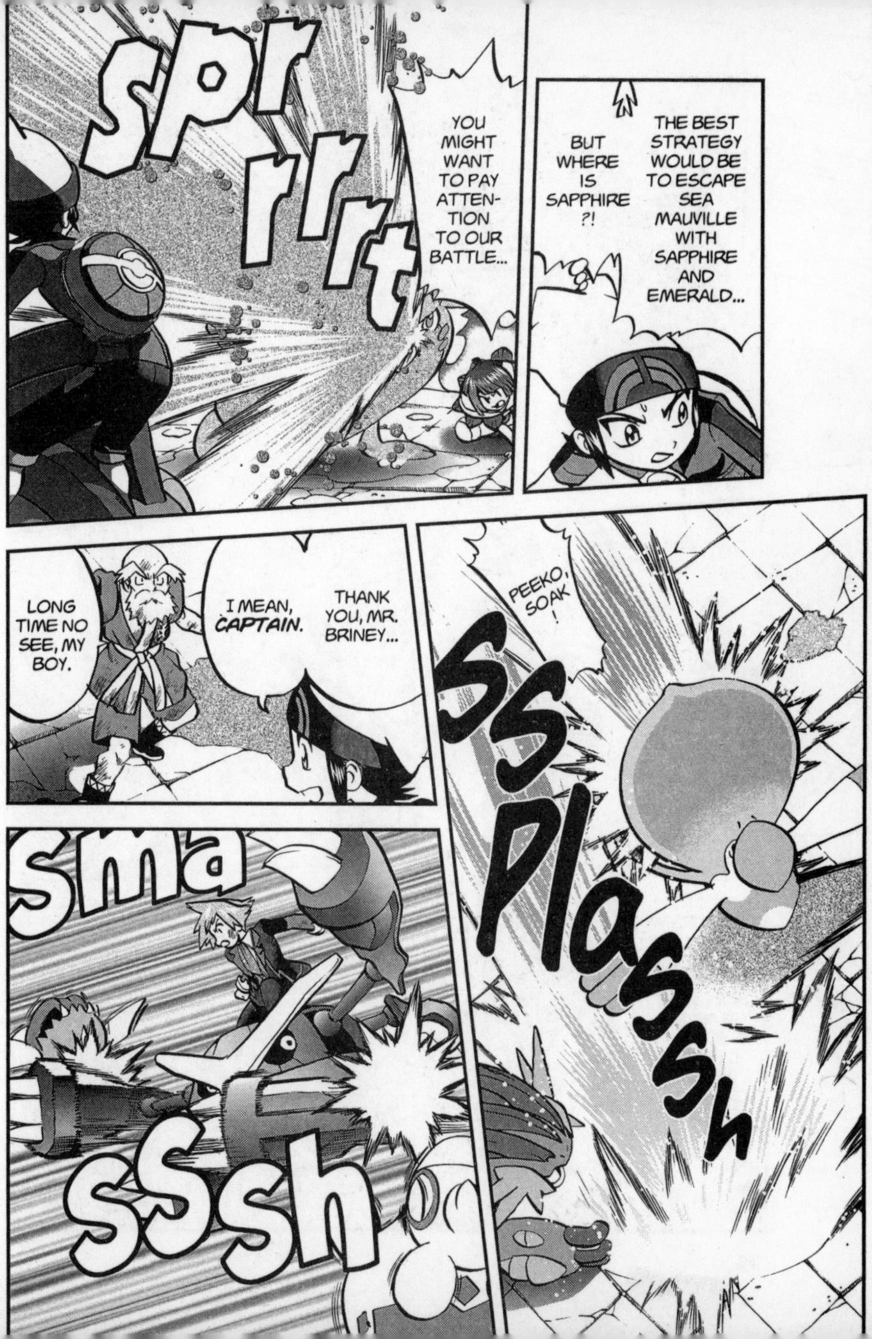
THE BEST STRATEGY WOULD BE TO ESCAPE SEA MAUVILLE WITH SAPPHIRE AND EMERALD...
BUT WHERE IS SAPPHIRE ?!
YOU MIGHT WANT TO PAY ATTENTION TO OUR BATTLE...
sprrrrt
PEEKO, SOAK!
SSPlasssh
THANK YOU, MR. BRINEY...
I MEAN, CAPTAIN.
LONG TIME NO SEE, MY BOY.
sma
sSsh

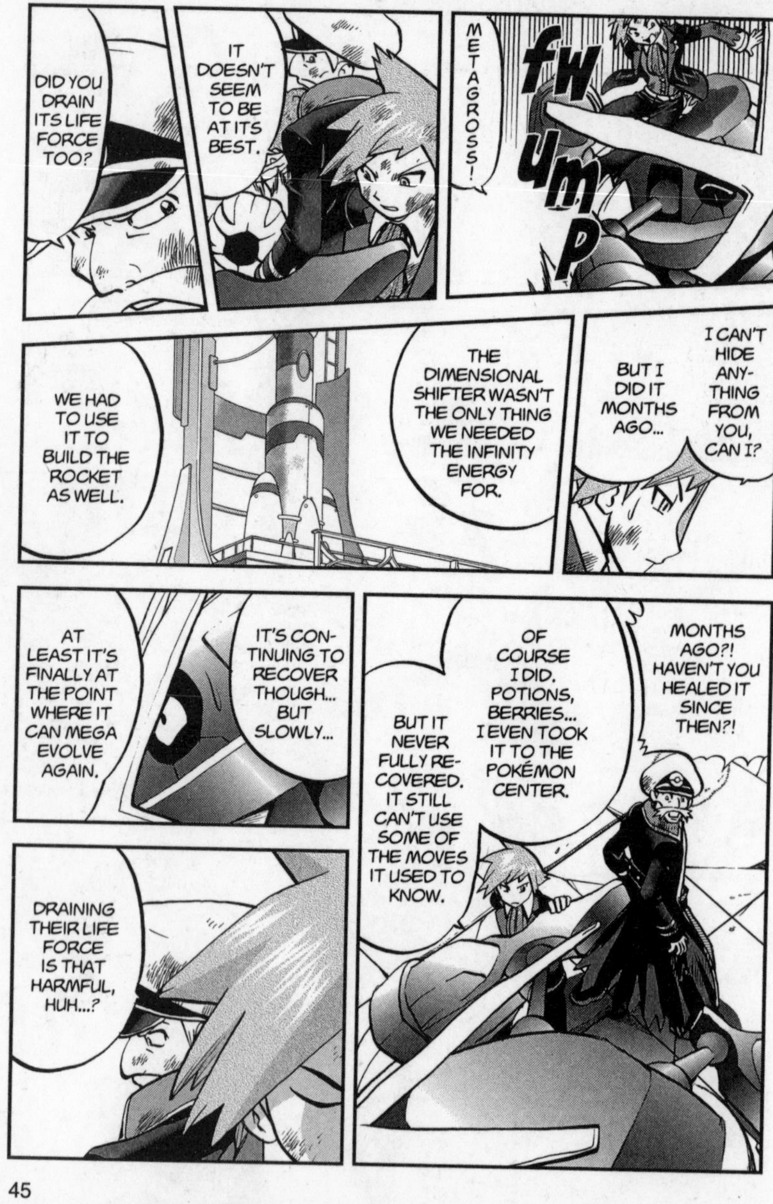
METAGROSS!
FWUMP
IT DOESN'T SEEM TO BE AT ITS BEST.
DID YOU DRAIN ITS LIFE FORCE TOO?
I CAN'T HIDE ANYTHING FROM YOU, CAN I?
BUT I DID IT MONTHS AGO...
THE DIMENSIONAL SHIFTER WASN'T THE ONLY THING WE NEEDED THE INFINITY ENERGY FOR.
WE HAD TO USE IT TO BUILD THE ROCKET AS WELL.
MONTHS AGO?! HAVEN'T YOU HEALED IT SINCE THEN?!
OF COURSE I DID. POTIONS, BERRIES... I EVEN TOOK IT TO THE POKÉMON CENTER.
BUT IT NEVER FULLY RE-COVERED. IT STILL CAN'T USE SOME OF THE MOVES IT USED TO KNOW.
IT'S CON-TINUING TO RECOVER THOUGH... BUT SLOWLY...
AT LEAST IT'S FINALLY AT THE POINT WHERE IT CAN MEGA EVOLVE AGAIN.
DRAINING THEIR LIFE FORCE IS THAT HARMFUL, HUH...?

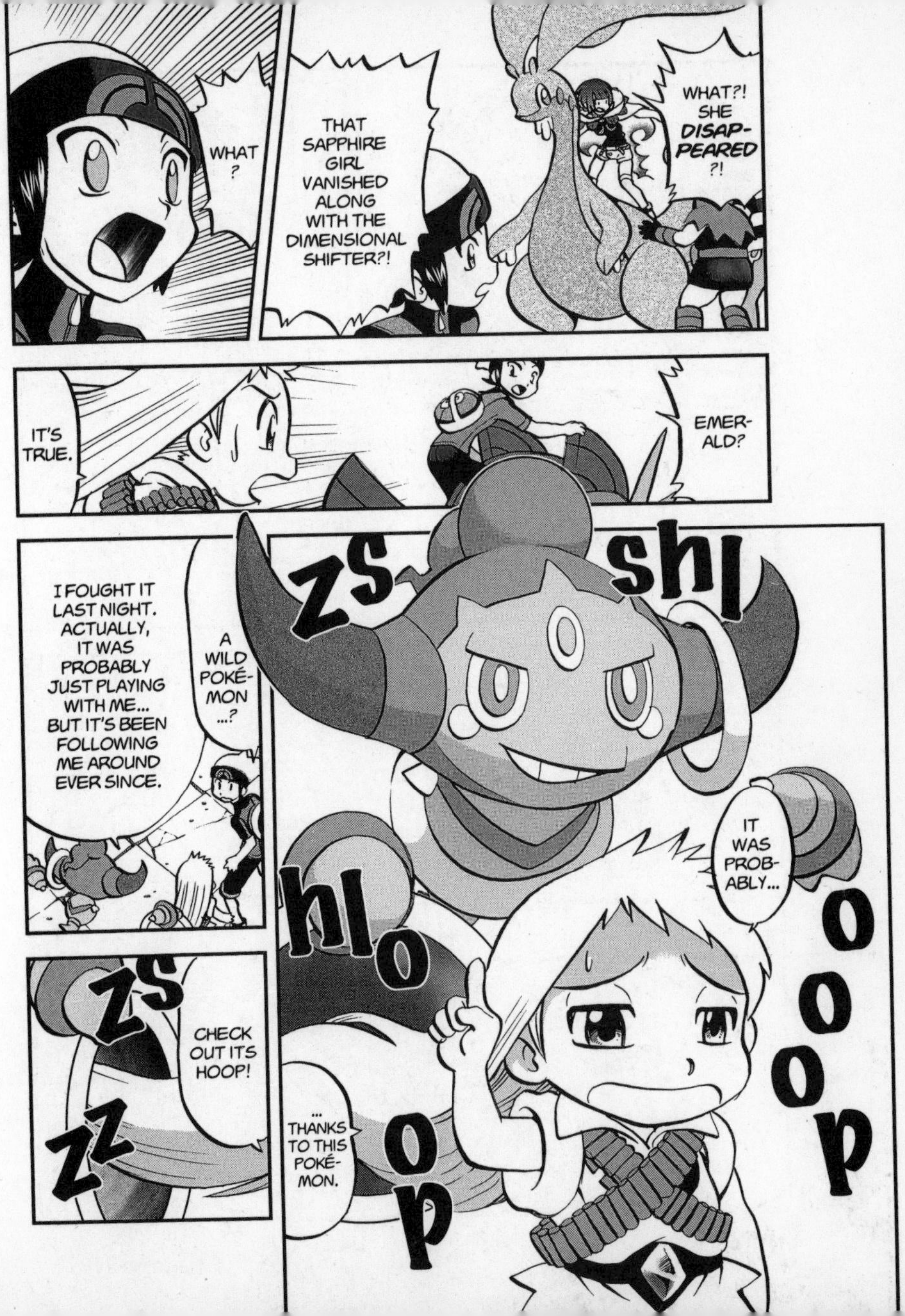
WHAT?! SHE DISAPPEARED?!
THAT SAPPHIRE GIRL VANISHED ALONG WITH THE DIMENSIONAL SHIFTER?!
WHAT?
EMERALD?
IT'S TRUE.
ZS SHL
IT WAS PROBABLY...
HLO
OOOOP
... THANKS TO THIS POKÉMON.
OP
A WILD POKÉMON ...?
I FOUGHT IT LAST NIGHT. ACTUALLY, IT WAS PROBABLY JUST PLAYING WITH ME... BUT IT'S BEEN FOLLOWING ME AROUND EVER SINCE.
ZS
CHECK OUT ITS HOOP!
ZZ

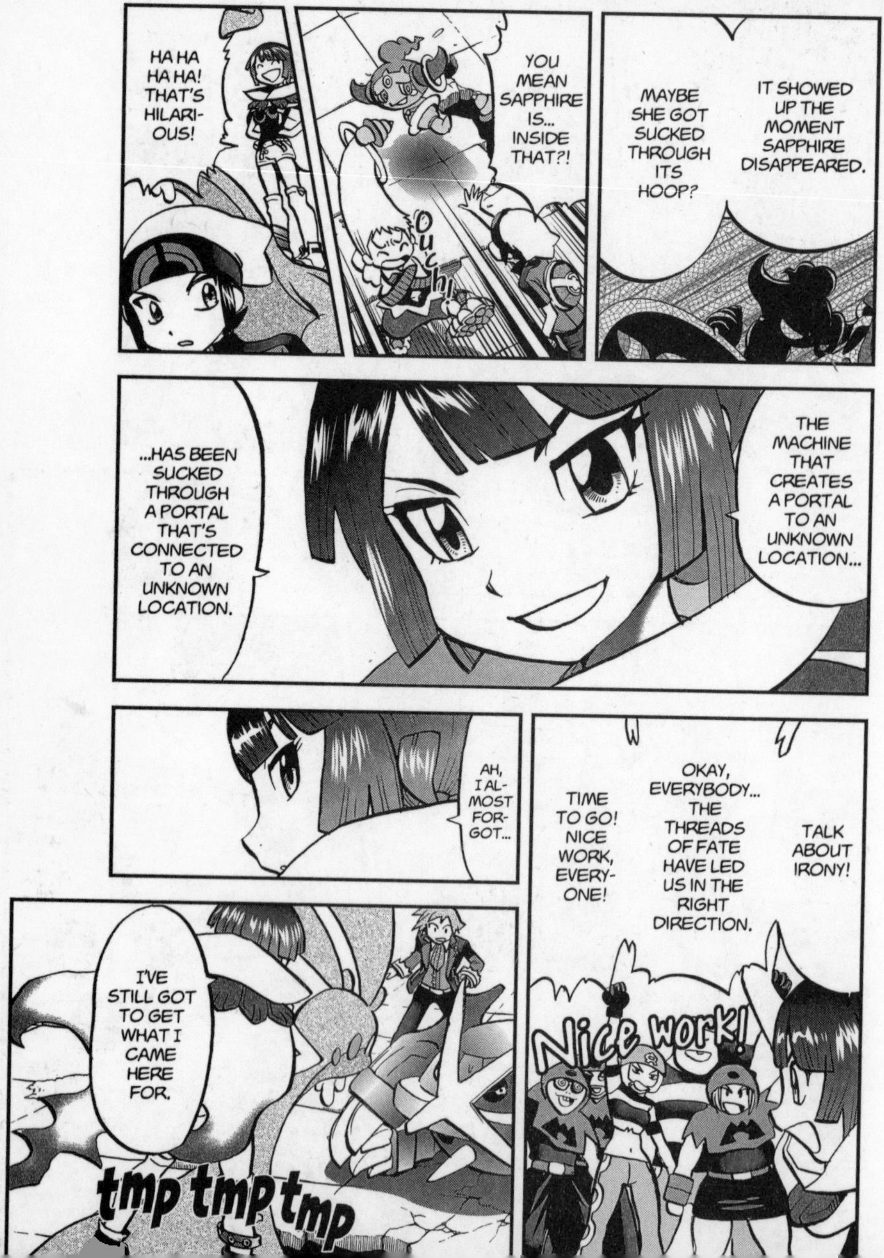
IT SHOWED UP THE MOMENT SAPPHIRE DISAPPEARED.
MAYBE SHE GOT SUCKED THROUGH ITS HOOP?
YOU MEAN SAPPHIRE IS... INSIDE THAT?!
Ouch!
HA HA HA HA! THAT'S HILARIOUS!
THE MACHINE THAT CREATES A PORTAL TO AN UNKNOWN LOCATION...
...HAS BEEN SUCKED THROUGH A PORTAL THAT'S CONNECTED TO AN UNKNOWN LOCATION.
TALK ABOUT IRONY!
OKAY, EVERYBODY... THE THREADS OF FATE HAVE LED US IN THE RIGHT DIRECTION.
TIME TO GO! NICE WORK, EVERYONE!
Nice work!
AH, I ALMOST FORGOT...
I'VE STILL GOT TO GET WHAT I CAME HERE FOR.
tmp tmp tmp

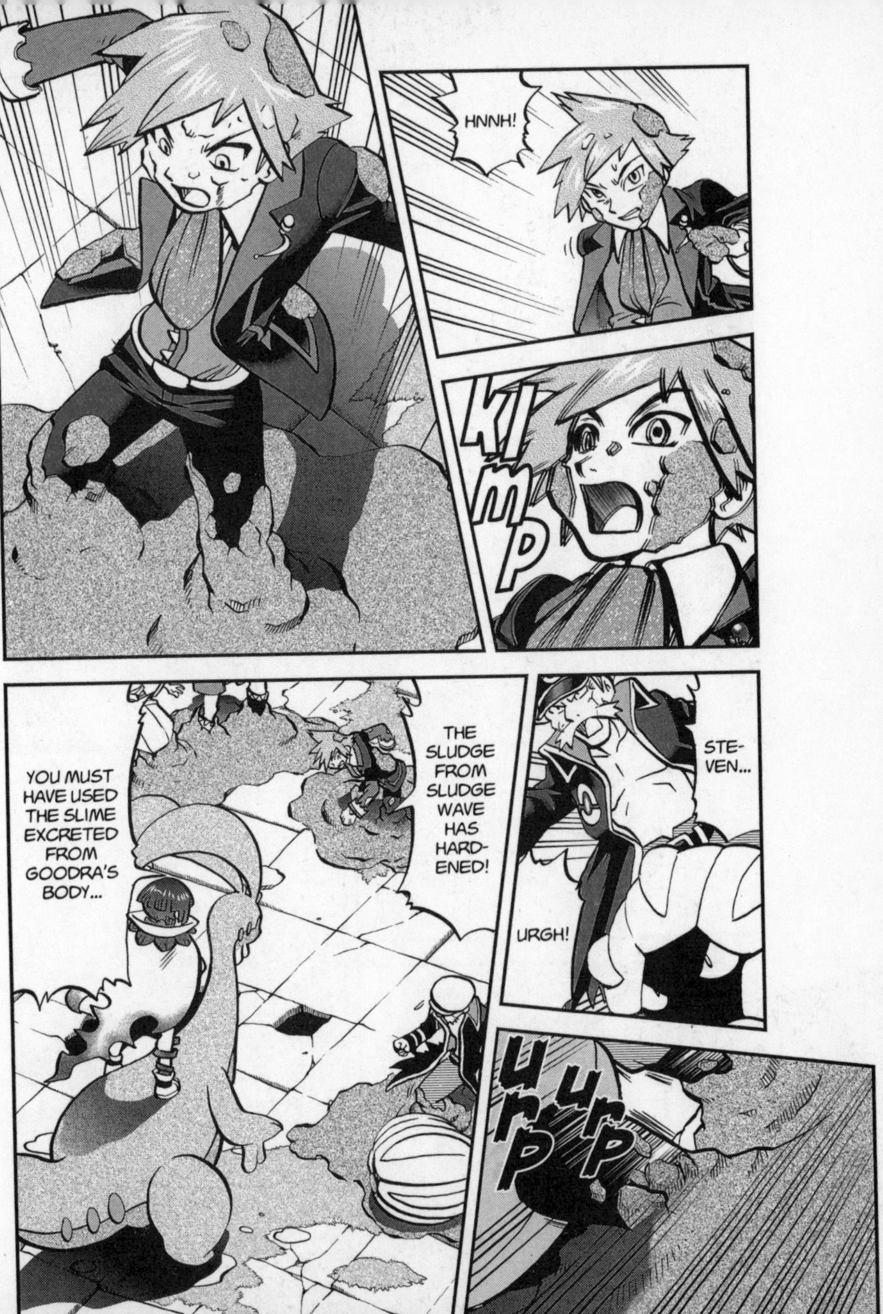
HNNH!
KLIMP
STE-VEN...
URGH!
URP URP
THE SLUDGE FROM SLUDGE WAVE HAS HARD-ENED!
YOU MUST HAVE USED THE SLIME EXCRETED FROM GOODRA'S BODY...

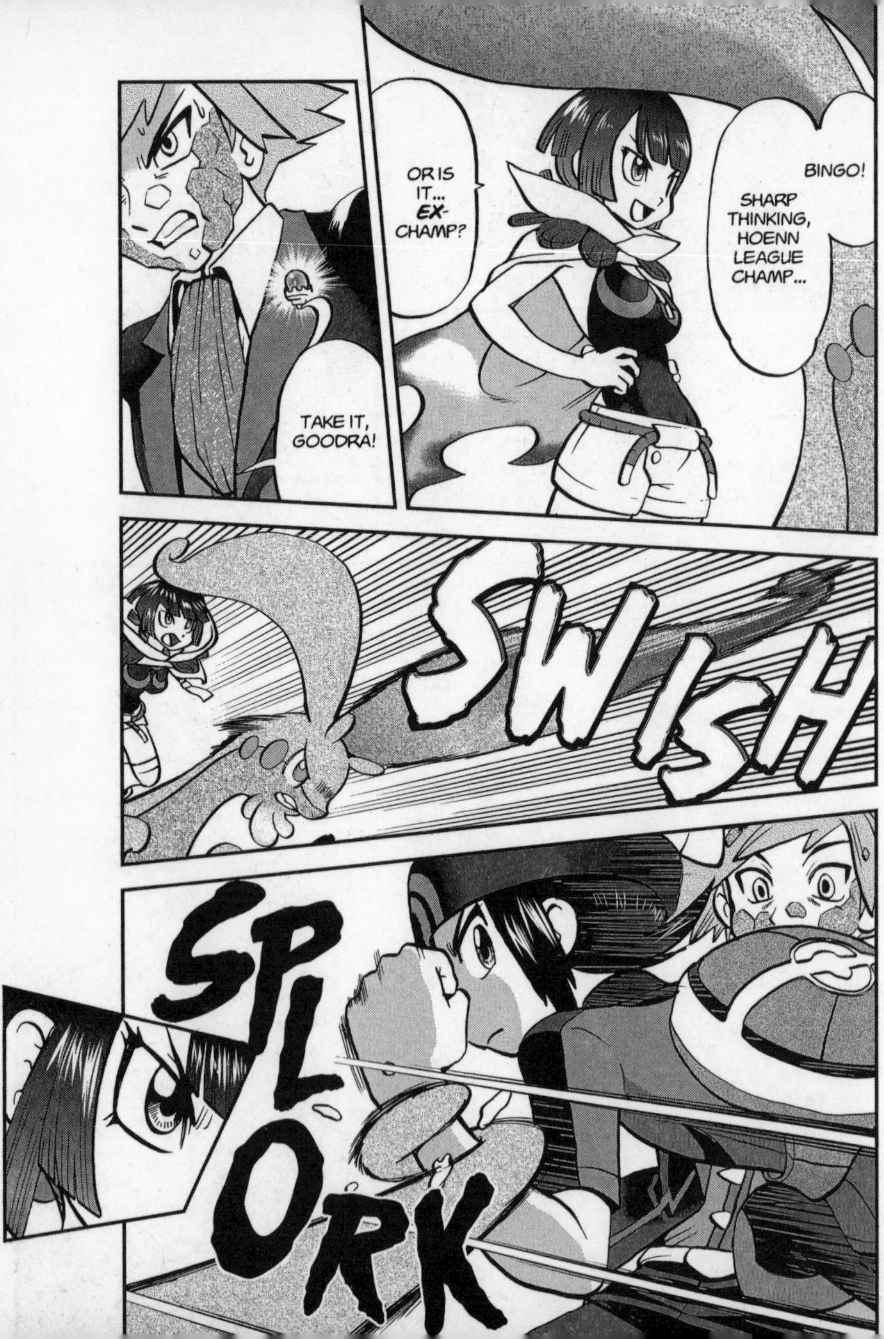
BINGO!
SHARP THINKING, HOENN LEAGUE CHAMP...
OR IS IT... EX-CHAMP?
TAKE IT, GOODRA!
SWISH
SPLORK

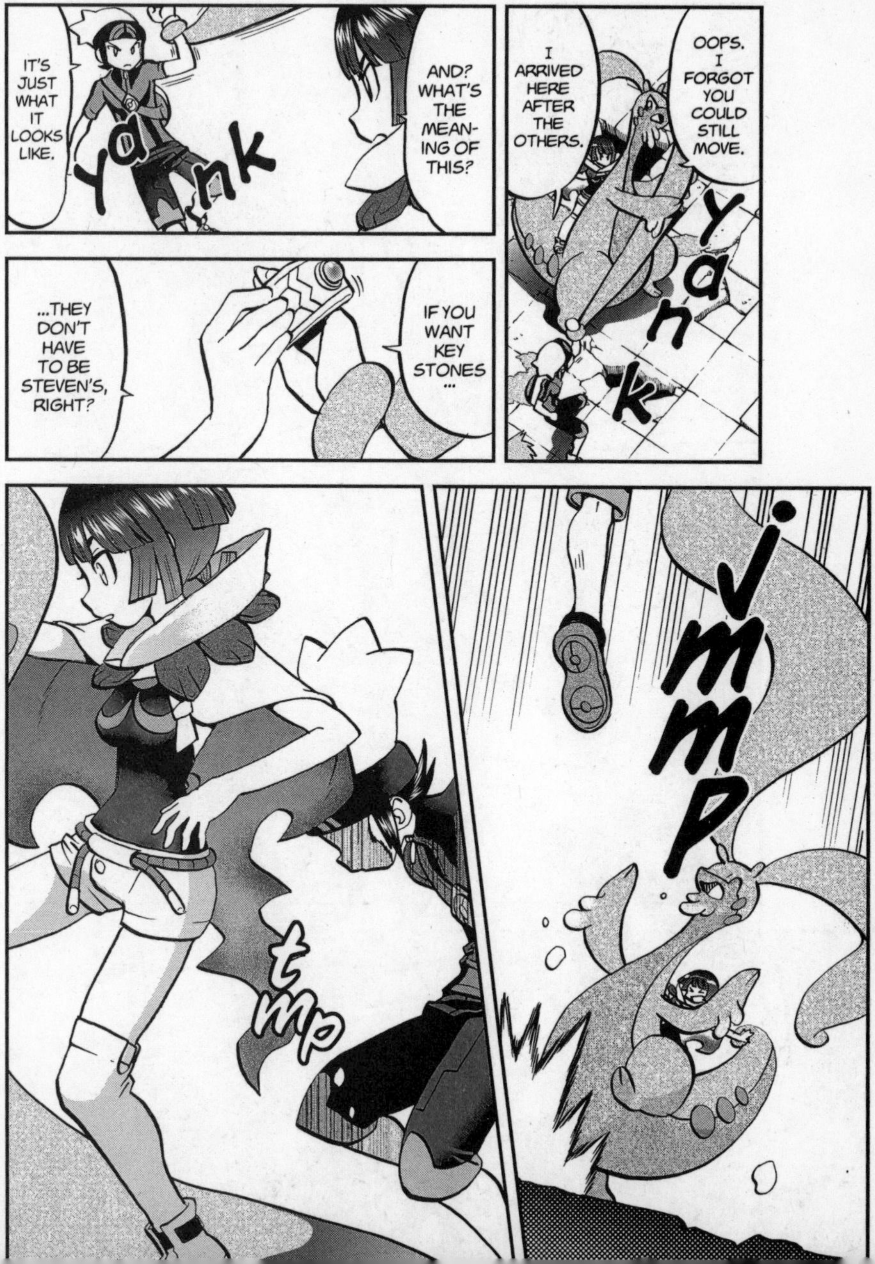
OOPS. I FORGOT YOU COULD STILL MOVE.
I ARRIVED HERE AFTER THE OTHERS.
Yank
AND? WHAT'S THE MEANING OF THIS?
IT'S JUST WHAT IT LOOKS LIKE.
Yank
IF YOU WANT KEY STONES...
...THEY DON'T HAVE TO BE STEVEN'S, RIGHT?
jMMP!
tmp

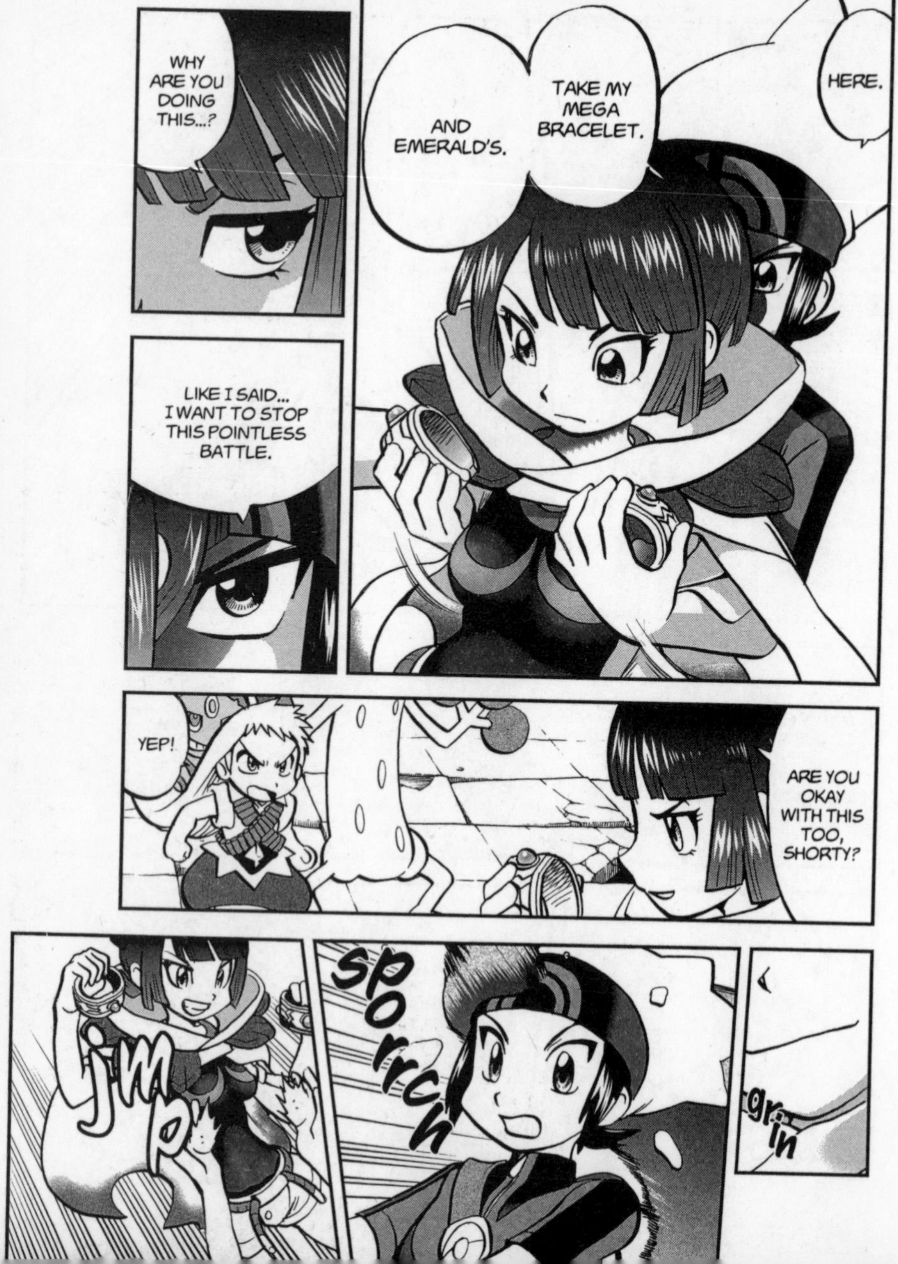
HERE.
TAKE MY MEGA BRACELET.
AND EMERALD'S.
WHY ARE YOU DOING THIS...?
LIKE I SAID... I WANT TO STOP THIS POINTLESS BATTLE.
ARE YOU OKAY WITH THIS TOO, SHORTY?
YEP!
grin

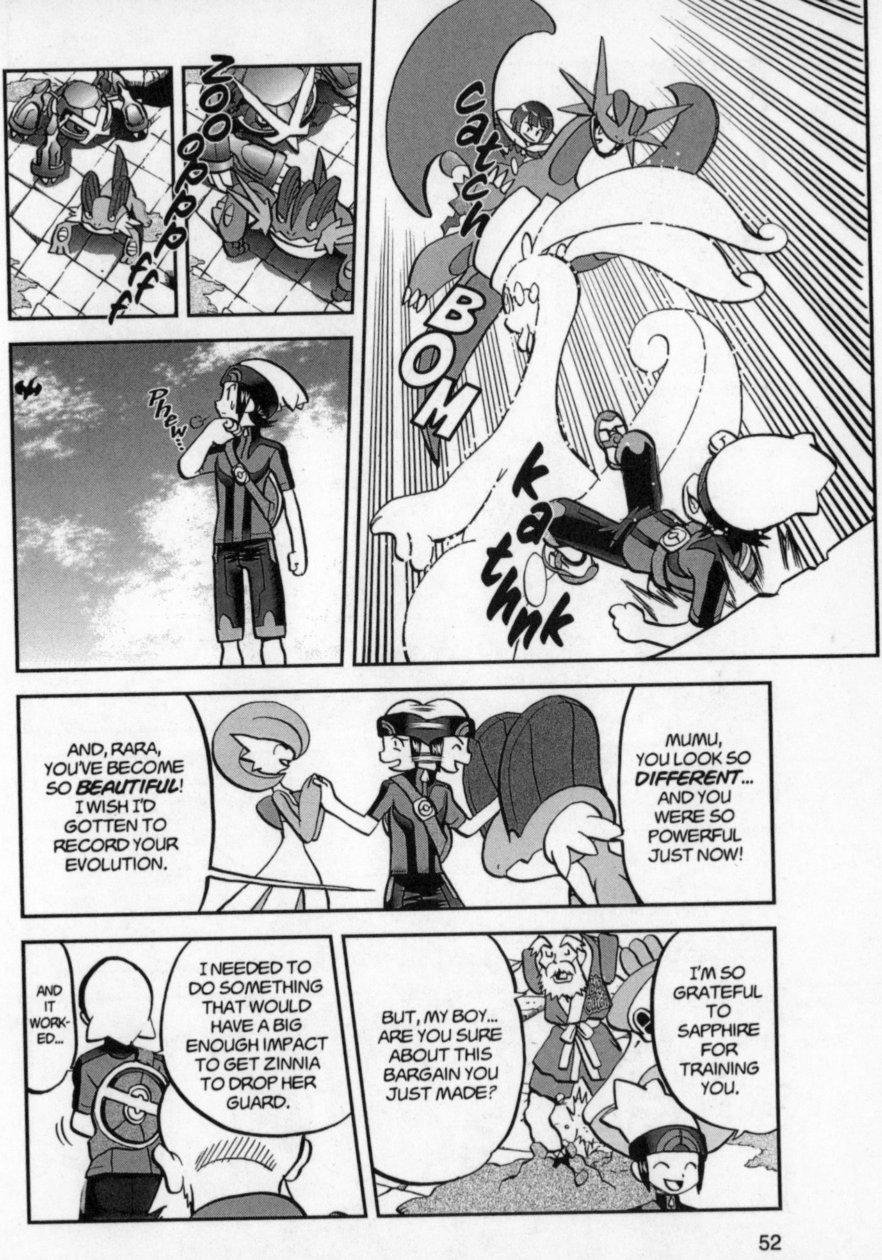
catch
BOM
ka thnk
ZOOOOPPPffff
Phew...
MUMU, YOU LOOK SO **DIFFERENT**... AND YOU WERE SO POWERFUL JUST NOW!
AND, RARA, YOU'VE BECOME SO **BEAUTIFUL**! I WISH I'D GOTTEN TO RECORD YOUR EVOLUTION.
I'M SO GRATEFUL TO SAPPHIRE FOR TRAINING YOU.
BUT, MY BOY... ARE YOU SURE ABOUT THIS BARGAIN YOU JUST MADE?
Big Catch
I NEEDED TO DO SOMETHING THAT WOULD HAVE A BIG ENOUGH IMPACT TO GET ZINNIA TO DROP HER GUARD.
AND IT WORK-ED...

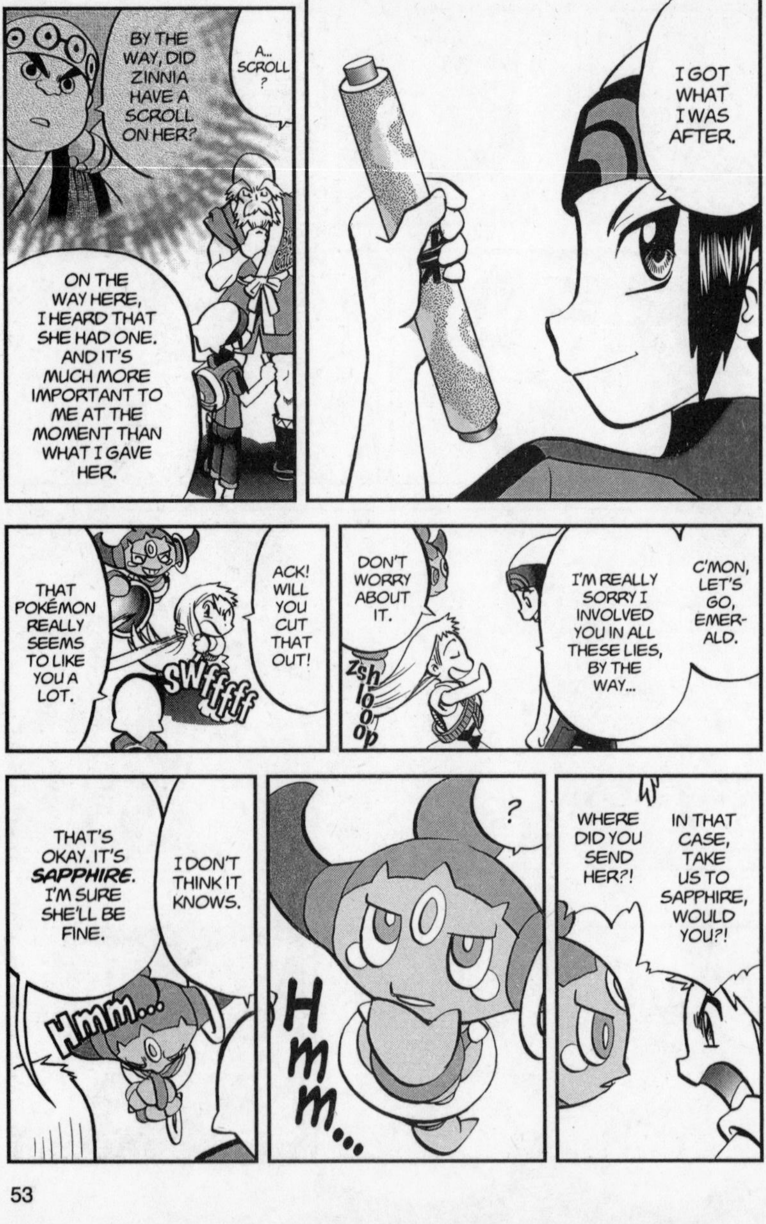
I GOT WHAT I WAS AFTER.
A... SCROLL?
BY THE WAY, DID ZINNIA HAVE A SCROLL ON HER?
ON THE WAY HERE, I HEARD THAT SHE HAD ONE. AND IT'S MUCH MORE IMPORTANT TO ME AT THE MOMENT THAN WHAT I GAVE HER.
C'MON, LET'S GO, EMERALD.
I'M REALLY SORRY I INVOLVED YOU IN ALL THESE LIES, BY THE WAY...
DON'T WORRY ABOUT IT.
Zshlooop
ACK! WILL YOU CUT THAT OUT!
THAT POKÉMON REALLY SEEMS TO LIKE YOU A LOT.
SWfffff
IN THAT CASE, TAKE US TO SAPPHIRE, WOULD YOU?!
WHERE DID YOU SEND HER?!
?
Hmm...
I DON'T THINK IT KNOWS.
THAT'S OKAY. IT'S ***SAPPHIRE***. I'M SURE SHE'LL BE FINE.
Hmm...

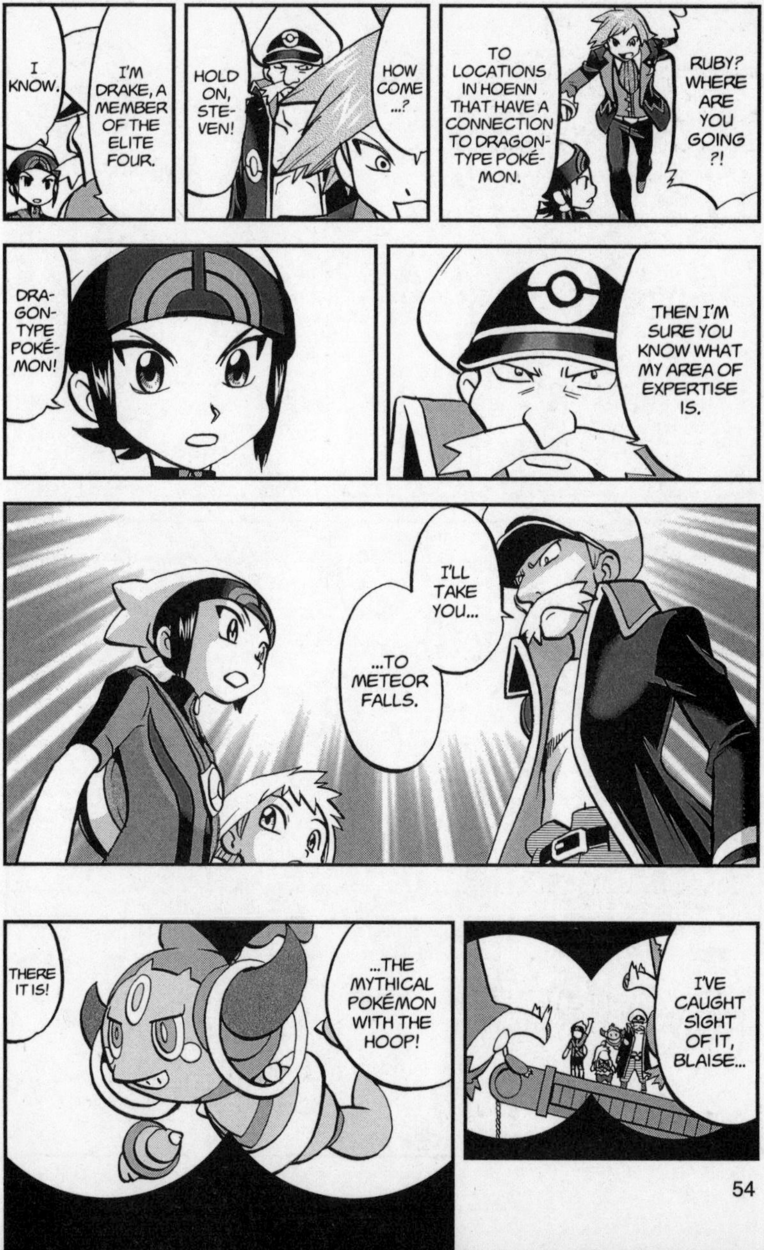
RUBY? WHERE ARE YOU GOING?!
TO LOCATIONS IN HOENN THAT HAVE A CONNECTION TO DRAGON-TYPE POKÉMON.
HOW COME...?
HOLD ON, STEVEN!
I'M DRAKE, A MEMBER OF THE ELITE FOUR.
I KNOW.
THEN I'M SURE YOU KNOW WHAT MY AREA OF EXPERTISE IS.
DRAGON-TYPE POKÉMON!
I'LL TAKE YOU...
...TO METEOR FALLS.
I'VE CAUGHT SIGHT OF IT, BLAISE...
...THE MYTHICAL POKÉMON WITH THE HOOP!
THERE IT IS!

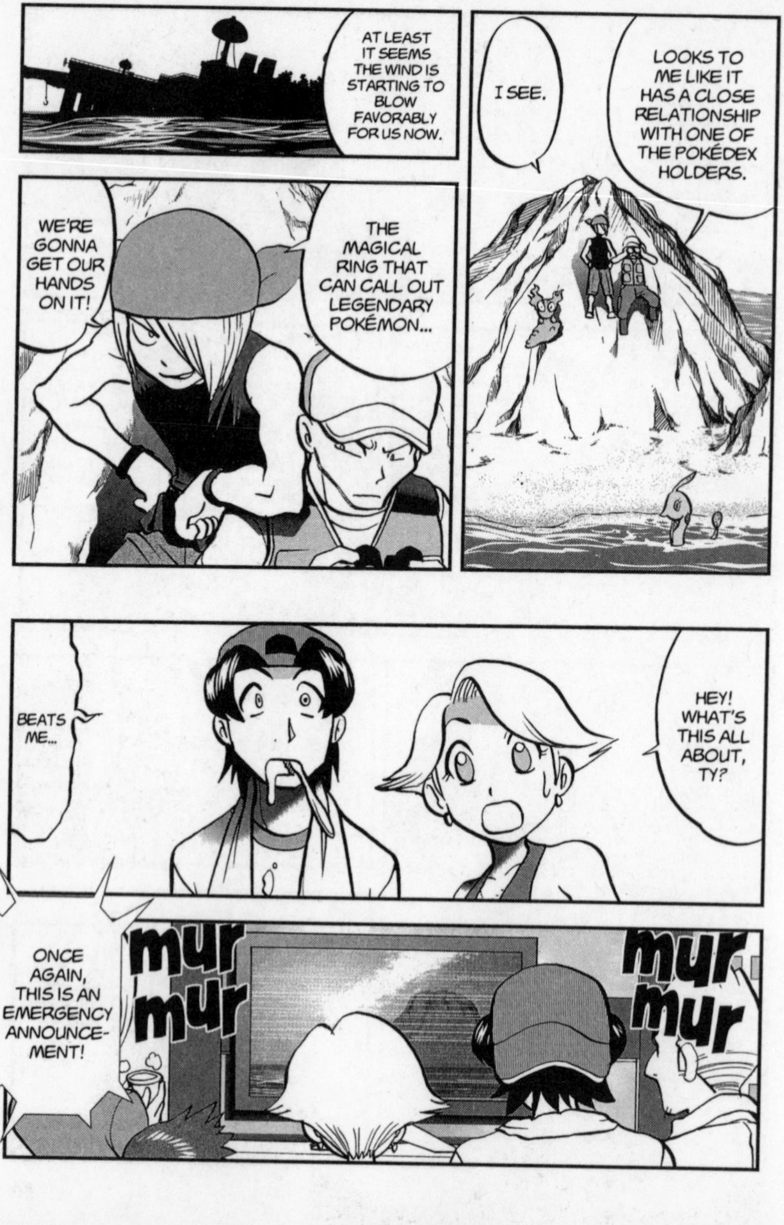
LOOKS TO ME LIKE IT HAS A CLOSE RELATIONSHIP WITH ONE OF THE POKÉDEX HOLDERS.
I SEE.
AT LEAST IT SEEMS THE WIND IS STARTING TO BLOW FAVORABLY FOR US NOW.
THE MAGICAL RING THAT CAN CALL OUT LEGENDARY POKÉMON...
WE'RE GONNA GET OUR HANDS ON IT!
HEY! WHAT'S THIS ALL ABOUT, TY?
BEATS ME...
mur mur
ONCE AGAIN, THIS IS AN EMERGENCY ANNOUNCE-MENT!
mur mur

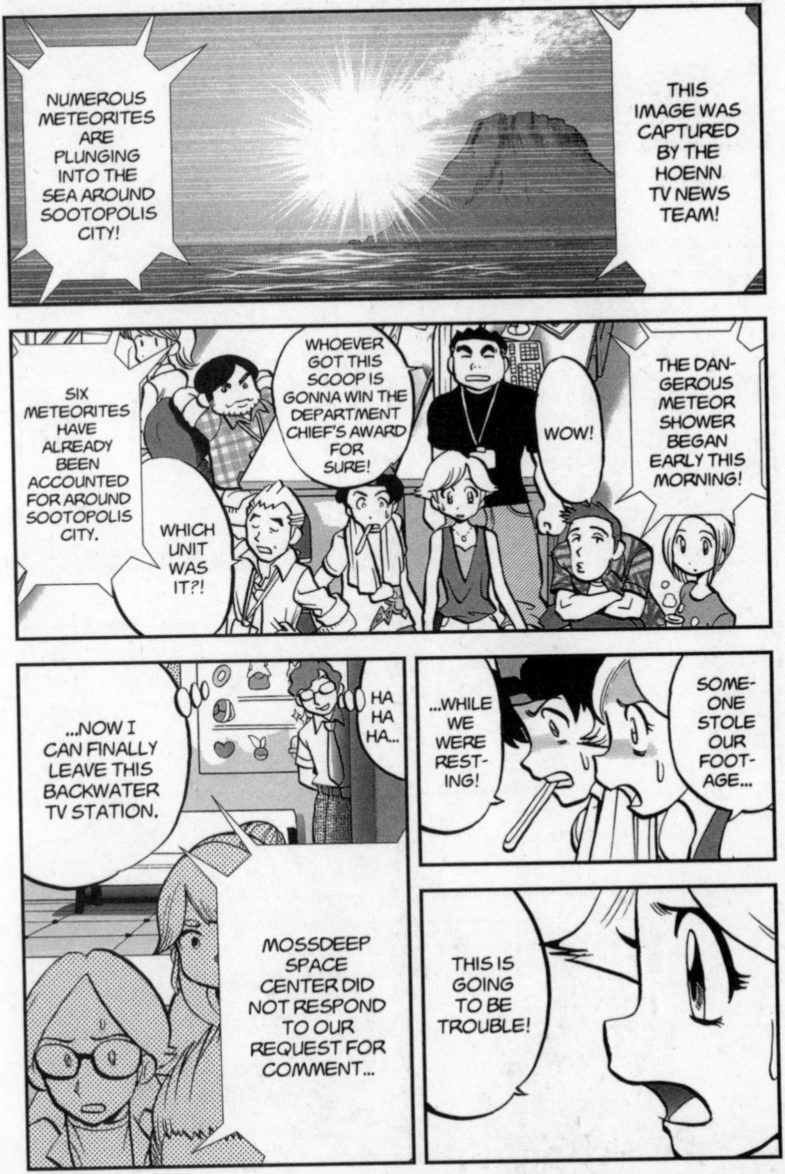
THIS IMAGE WAS CAPTURED BY THE HOENN TV NEWS TEAM!
NUMEROUS METEORITES ARE PLUNGING INTO THE SEA AROUND SOOTOPOLIS CITY!
THE DANGEROUS METEOR SHOWER BEGAN EARLY THIS MORNING!
WOW!
WHOEVER GOT THIS SCOOP IS GONNA WIN THE DEPARTMENT CHIEF'S AWARD FOR SURE!
SIX METEORITES HAVE ALREADY BEEN ACCOUNTED FOR AROUND SOOTOPOLIS CITY.
WHICH UNIT WAS IT?!
SOMEONE STOLE OUR FOOTAGE...
...WHILE WE WERE RESTING!
THIS IS GOING TO BE TROUBLE!
HA HA HA...
...NOW I CAN FINALLY LEAVE THIS BACKWATER TV STATION.
MOSSDEEP SPACE CENTER DID NOT RESPOND TO OUR REQUEST FOR COMMENT...

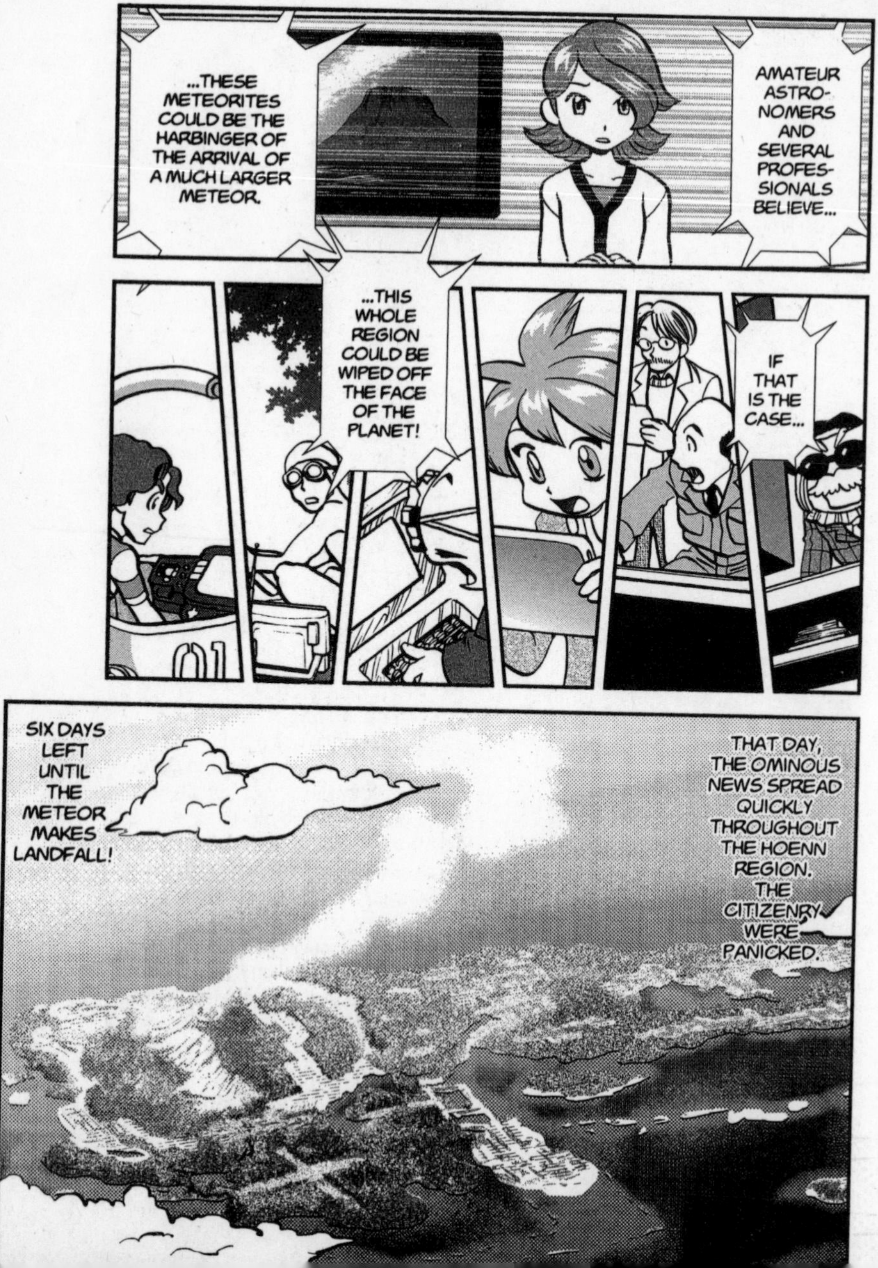
AMATEUR ASTRONOMERS AND SEVERAL PROFESSIONALS BELIEVE...
...THESE METEORITES COULD BE THE HARBINGER OF THE ARRIVAL OF A MUCH LARGER METEOR.
IF THAT IS THE CASE...
...THIS WHOLE REGION COULD BE WIPED OFF THE FACE OF THE PLANET!
THAT DAY, THE OMINOUS NEWS SPREAD QUICKLY THROUGHOUT THE HOENN REGION. THE CITIZENRY WERE PANICKED.
SIX DAYS LEFT UNTIL THE METEOR MAKES LANDFALL!

FORCE ABSORBER

The device that absorbs Pokémon life forces. It can absorb any life force and convert it into Infinity Energy.

DIMENSIONAL SHIFTER

A machine that will teleport an object from one place to another. It moves on Infinity Energy and was built by the Devon Corporation.

INFINITY ENERGY

An energy created by converting Pokémon life forces. It was put into practical use by the Devon Corporation's previous president, the grandfather of Steven Stone. The technology is based on an Ultimate Weapon created by a man in a certain region to stop the war, and the same mechanism is used to convert Pokémon life forces into Infinity Energy. Infinity Energy has been used for many things, such as the engine that propels the rocket into second cosmic velocity, as well as for the motor of Submarine Explorer 1. It was the success of this technology that enabled the Devon Corporation to become the leading firm at Hoenn.

Omega Alpha Adventure 10

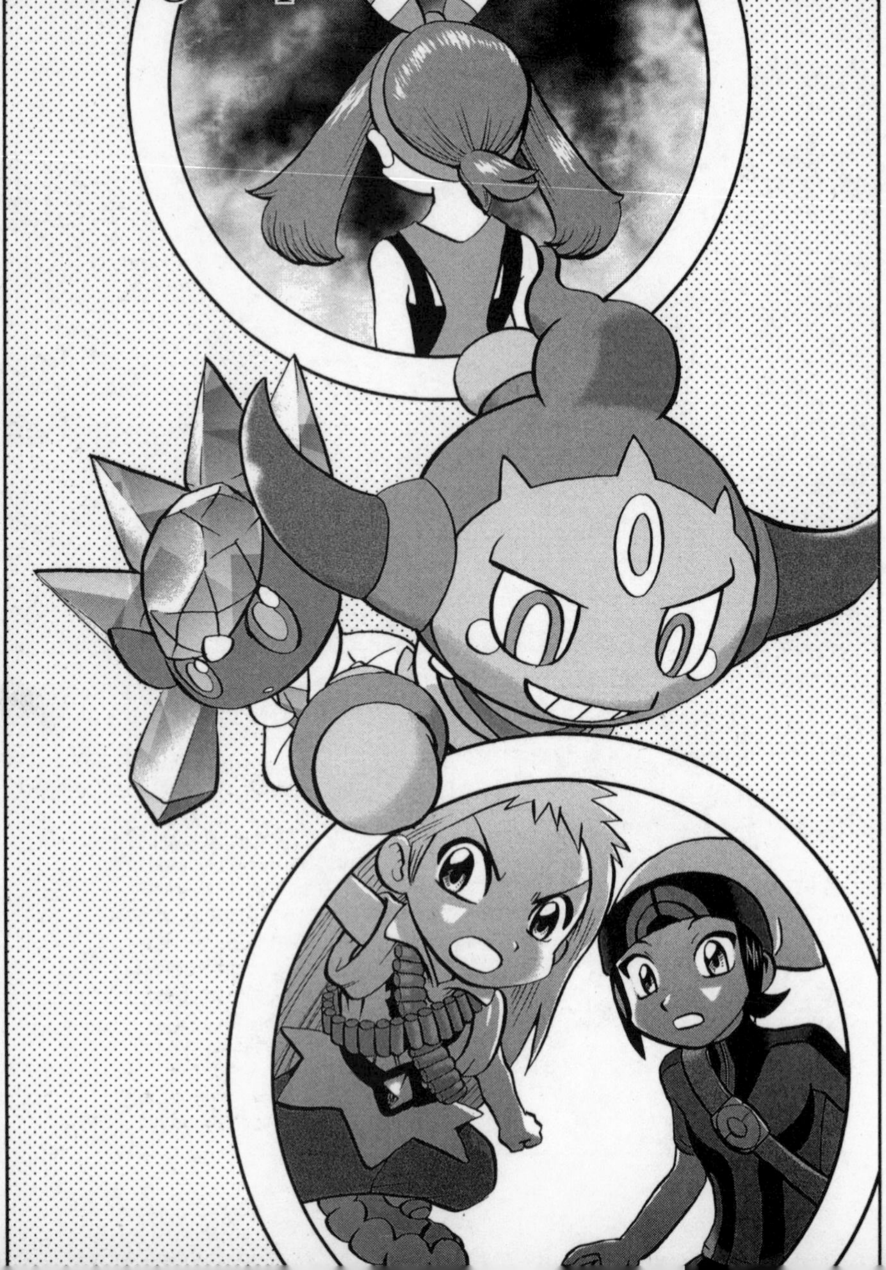

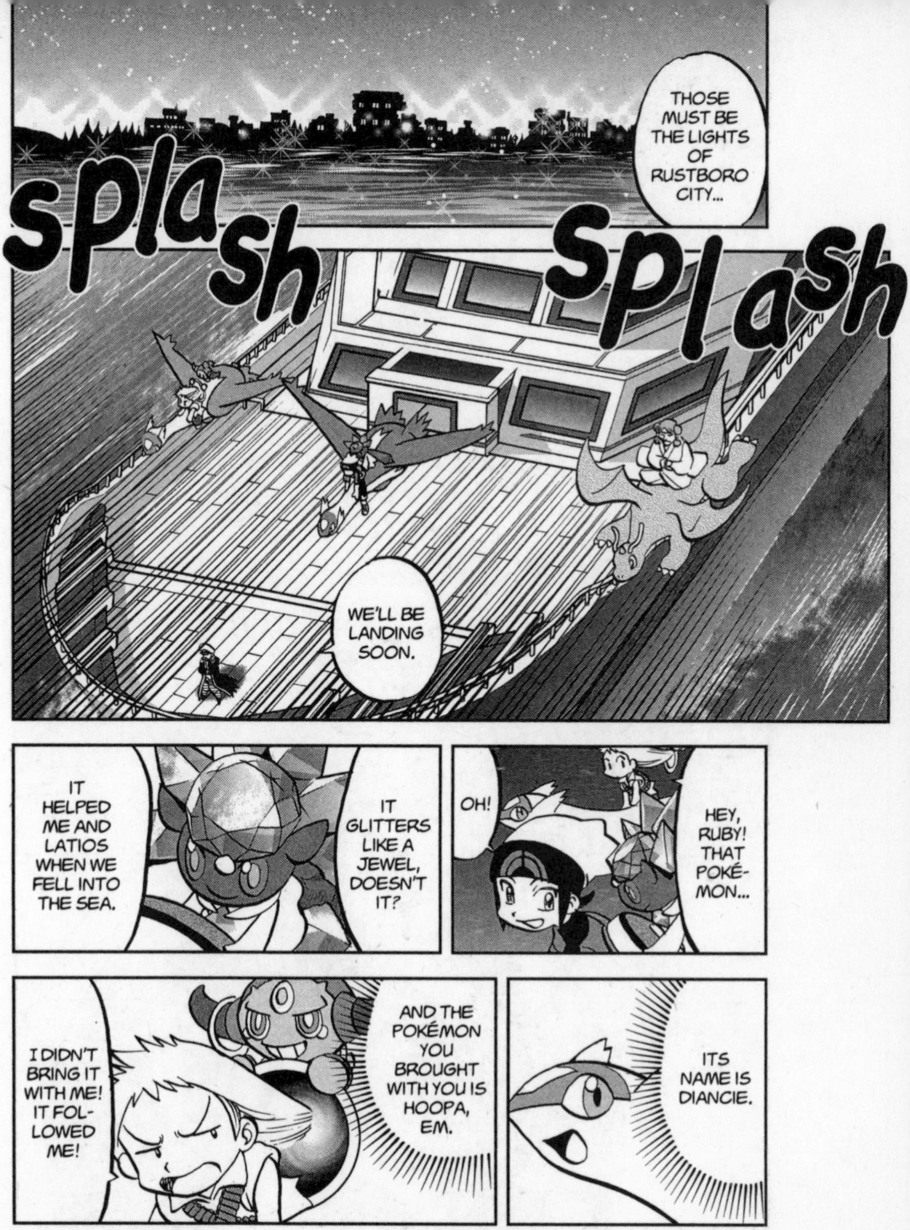
THOSE MUST BE THE LIGHTS OF RUSTBORO CITY...
splash
splash
WE'LL BE LANDING SOON.
HEY, RUBY! THAT POKÉMON...
OH!
IT GLITTERS LIKE A JEWEL, DOESN'T IT?
IT HELPED ME AND LATIOS WHEN WE FELL INTO THE SEA.
ITS NAME IS DIANCIE.
AND THE POKÉMON YOU BROUGHT WITH YOU IS HOOPA, EM.
I DIDN'T BRING IT WITH ME! IT FOL-LOWED ME!

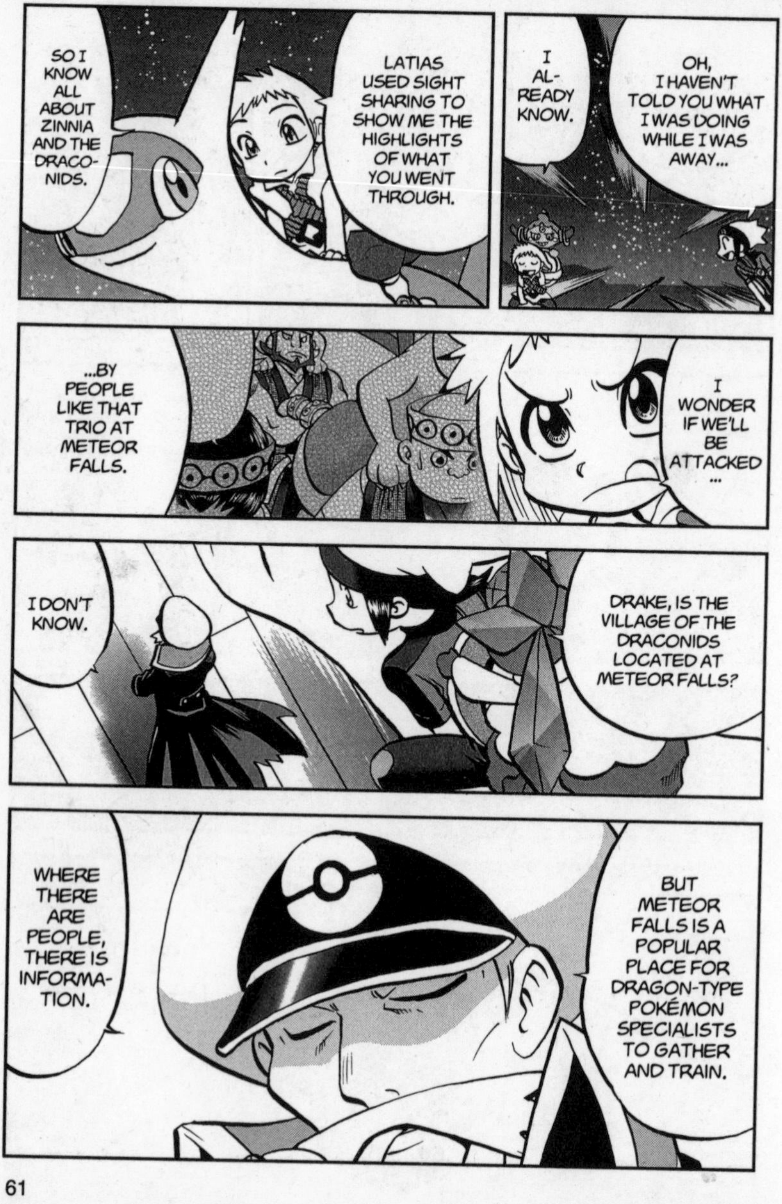
OH, I HAVEN'T TOLD YOU WHAT I WAS DOING WHILE I WAS AWAY...
I ALREADY KNOW.
LATIAS USED SIGHT SHARING TO SHOW ME THE HIGHLIGHTS OF WHAT YOU WENT THROUGH.
SO I KNOW ALL ABOUT ZINNIA AND THE DRACONIDS.
I WONDER IF WE'LL BE ATTACKED...
...BY PEOPLE LIKE THAT TRIO AT METEOR FALLS.
DRAKE, IS THE VILLAGE OF THE DRACONIDS LOCATED AT METEOR FALLS?
I DON'T KNOW.
BUT METEOR FALLS IS A POPULAR PLACE FOR DRAGON-TYPE POKÉMON SPECIALISTS TO GATHER AND TRAIN.
WHERE THERE ARE PEOPLE, THERE IS INFORMATION.

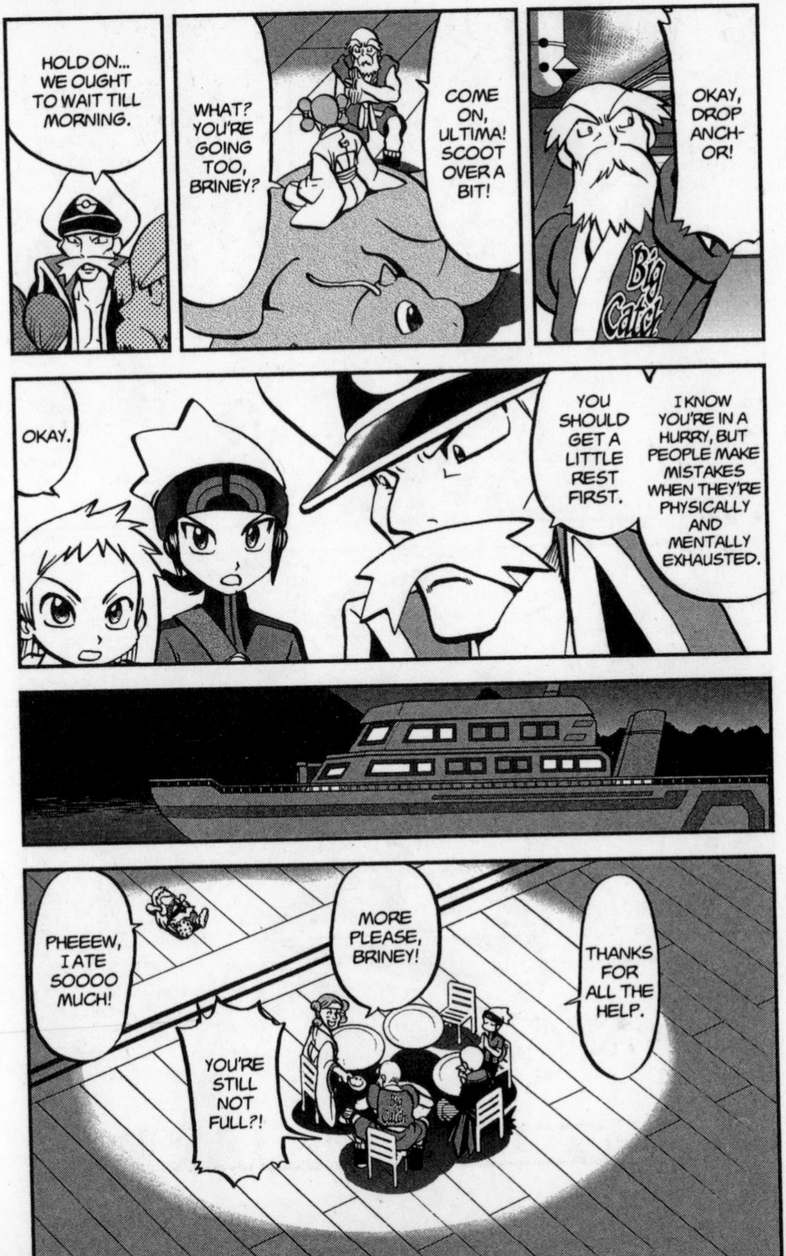
OKAY, DROP ANCHOR!
COME ON, ULTIMA! SCOOT OVER A BIT!
WHAT? YOU'RE GOING TOO, BRINEY?
HOLD ON... WE OUGHT TO WAIT TILL MORNING.
I KNOW YOU'RE IN A HURRY, BUT PEOPLE MAKE MISTAKES WHEN THEY'RE PHYSICALLY AND MENTALLY EXHAUSTED.
YOU SHOULD GET A LITTLE REST FIRST.
OKAY.
THANKS FOR ALL THE HELP.
MORE PLEASE, BRINEY!
PHEEEW, I ATE SOOOO MUCH!
YOU'RE STILL NOT FULL?!

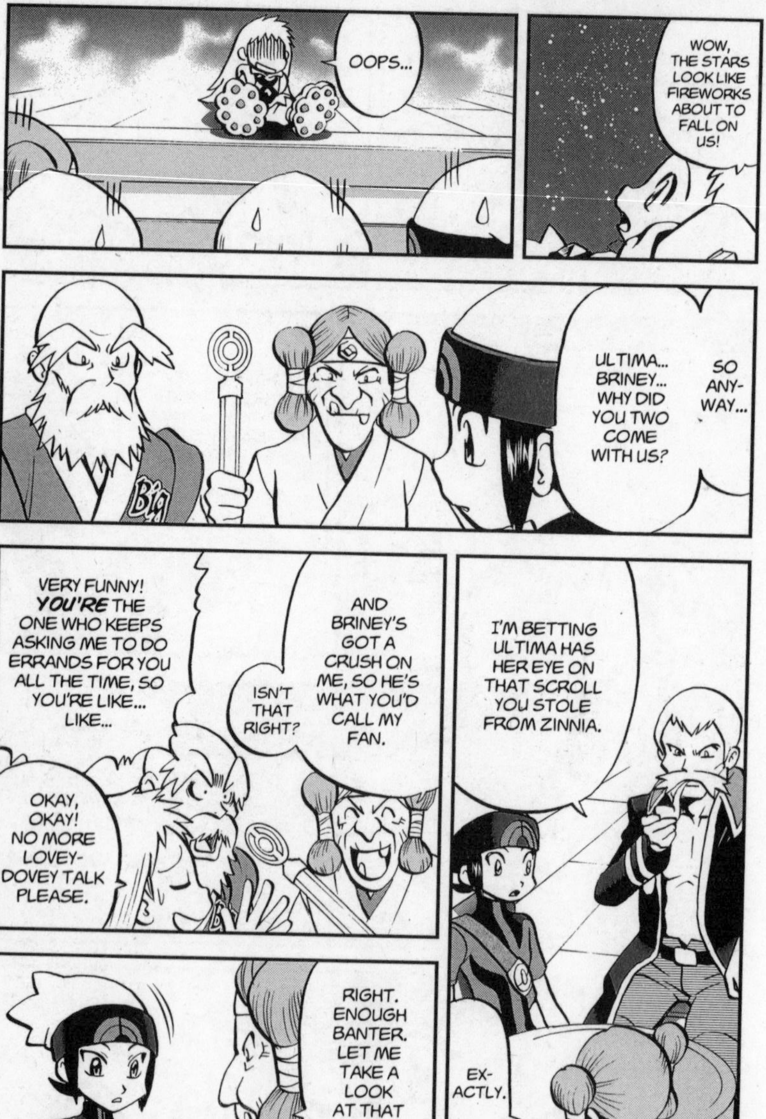
WOW, THE STARS LOOK LIKE FIREWORKS ABOUT TO FALL ON US!
OOPS...
SO ANYWAY...
ULTIMA... BRINEY... WHY DID YOU TWO COME WITH US?
I'M BETTING ULTIMA HAS HER EYE ON THAT SCROLL YOU STOLE FROM ZINNIA.
EX-ACTLY.
AND BRINEY'S GOT A CRUSH ON ME, SO HE'S WHAT YOU'D CALL MY FAN.
ISN'T THAT RIGHT?
VERY FUNNY! ***YOU'RE*** THE ONE WHO KEEPS ASKING ME TO DO ERRANDS FOR YOU ALL THE TIME, SO YOU'RE LIKE... LIKE...
OKAY, OKAY! NO MORE LOVEY-DOVEY TALK PLEASE.
RIGHT. ENOUGH BANTER. LET ME TAKE A LOOK AT THAT THING!

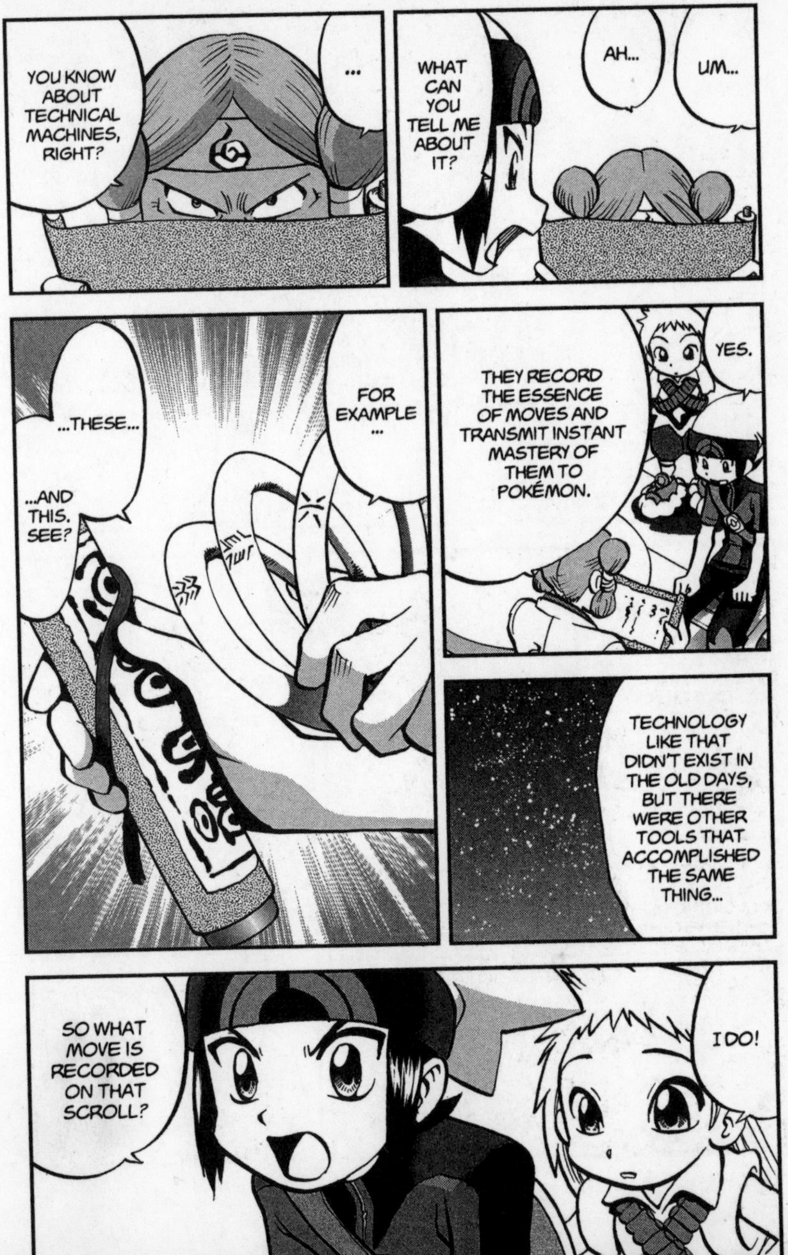
UM...
AH...
WHAT CAN YOU TELL ME ABOUT IT?
...
YOU KNOW ABOUT TECHNICAL MACHINES, RIGHT?
YES.
THEY RECORD THE ESSENCE OF MOVES AND TRANSMIT INSTANT MASTERY OF THEM TO POKÉMON.
TECHNOLOGY LIKE THAT DIDN'T EXIST IN THE OLD DAYS, BUT THERE WERE OTHER TOOLS THAT ACCOMPLISHED THE SAME THING...
FOR EXAMPLE ...
...THESE...
...AND THIS. SEE?
I DO!
SO WHAT MOVE IS RECORDED ON THAT SCROLL?

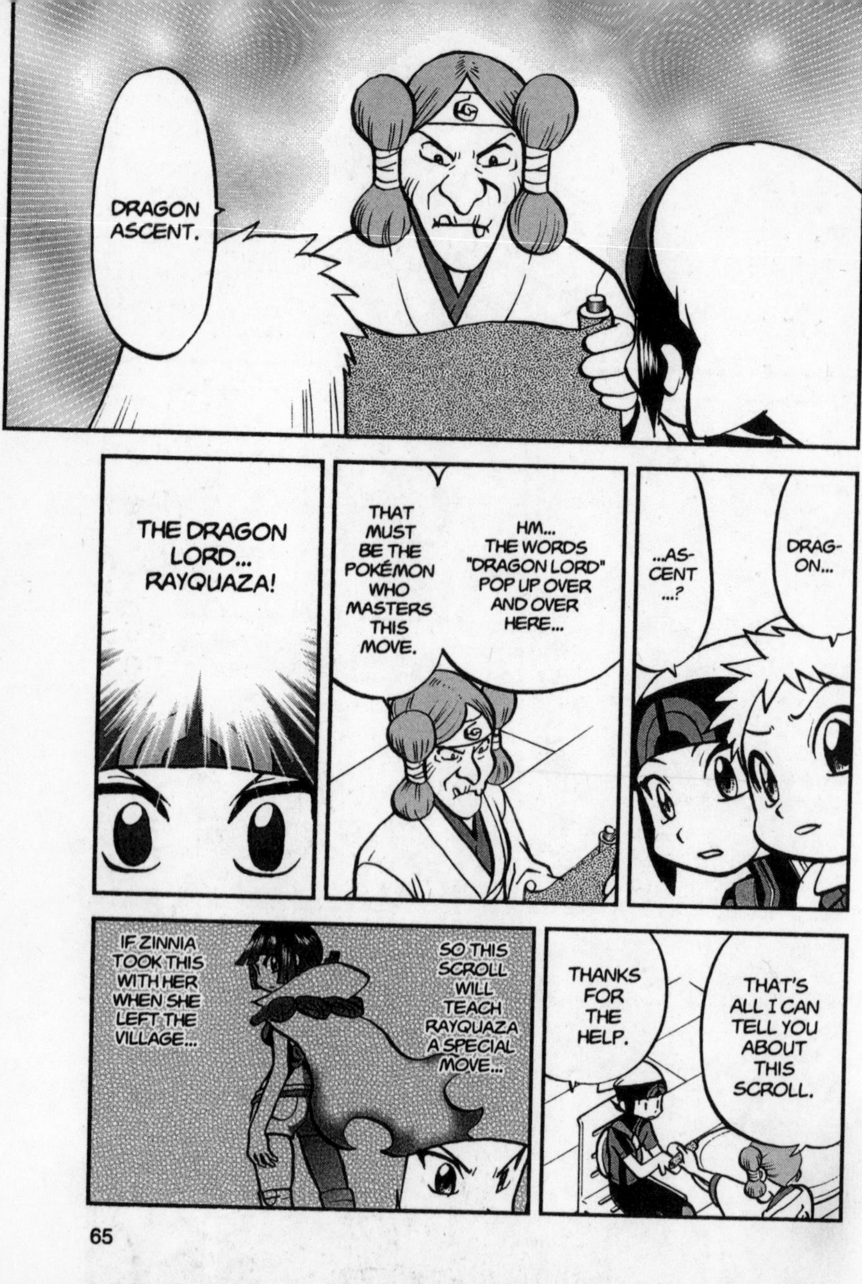
DRAGON ASCENT.
DRAG-ON...
...AS-CENT ...?
HM... THE WORDS "DRAGON LORD" POP UP OVER AND OVER HERE...
THAT MUST BE THE POKÉMON WHO MASTERS THIS MOVE.
THE DRAGON LORD... RAYQUAZA!
THAT'S ALL I CAN TELL YOU ABOUT THIS SCROLL.
THANKS FOR THE HELP.
SO THIS SCROLL WILL TEACH RAYQUAZA A SPECIAL MOVE...
IF ZINNIA TOOK THIS WITH HER WHEN SHE LEFT THE VILLAGE...

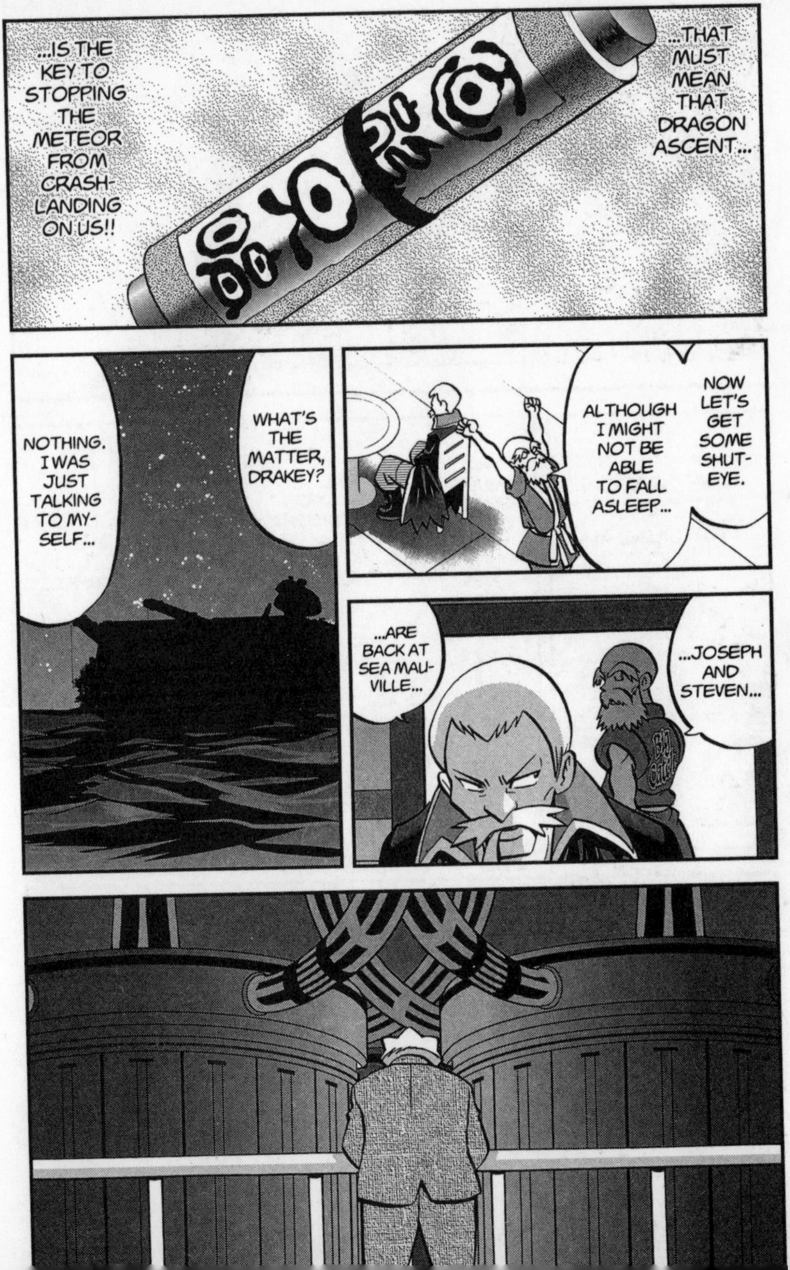
...THAT MUST MEAN THAT DRAGON ASCENT...
...IS THE KEY TO STOPPING THE METEOR FROM CRASH-LANDING ON US!!
NOW LET'S GET SOME SHUT-EYE.
ALTHOUGH I MIGHT NOT BE ABLE TO FALL ASLEEP...
...JOSEPH AND STEVEN...
...ARE BACK AT SEA MAUVILLE...
WHAT'S THE MATTER, DRAKEY?
NOTHING. I WAS JUST TALKING TO MYSELF...

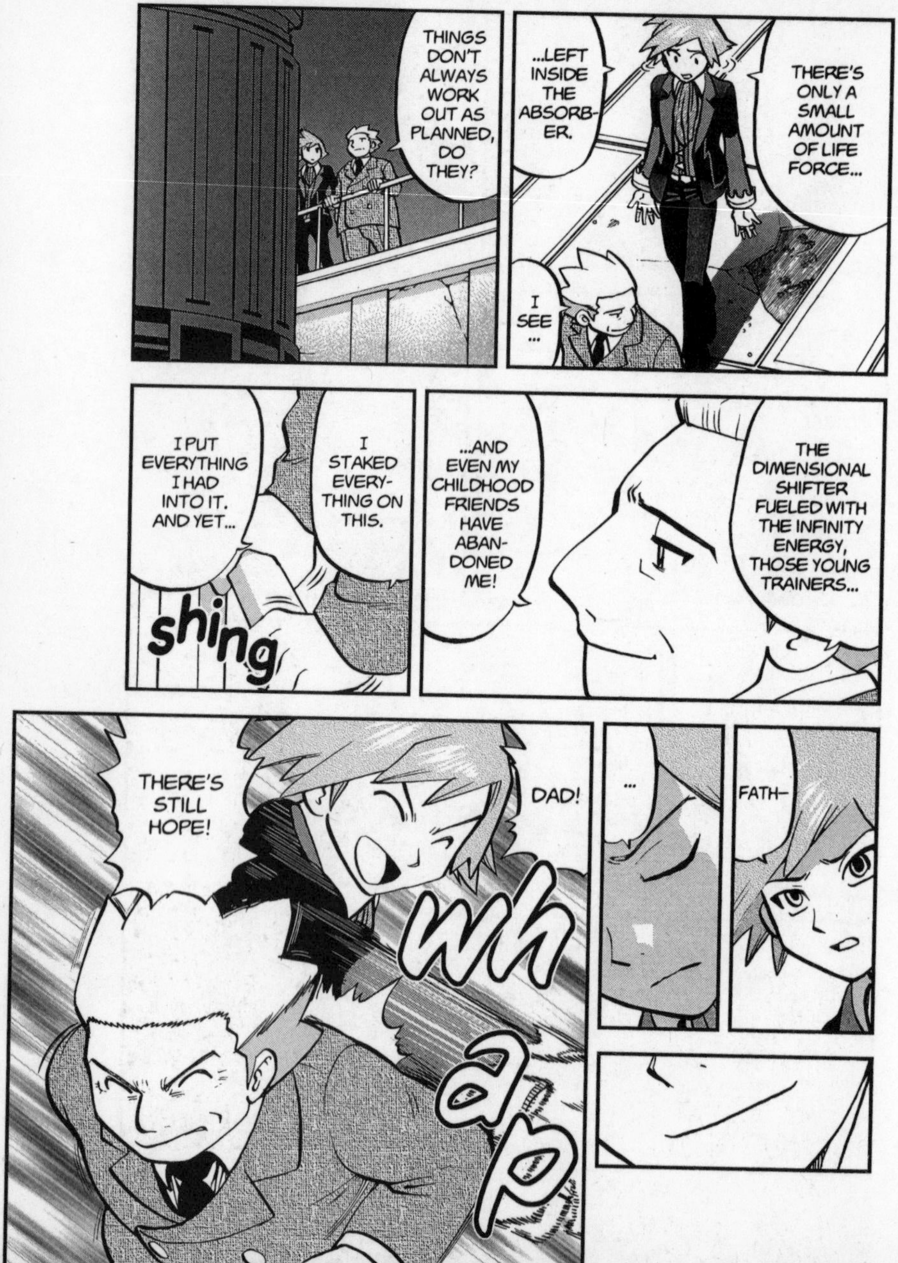
THERE'S ONLY A SMALL AMOUNT OF LIFE FORCE...
...LEFT INSIDE THE ABSORB-ER.
I SEE...
THINGS DON'T ALWAYS WORK OUT AS PLANNED, DO THEY?
THE DIMENSIONAL SHIFTER FUELED WITH THE INFINITY ENERGY, THOSE YOUNG TRAINERS...
...AND EVEN MY CHILDHOOD FRIENDS HAVE ABAN-DONED ME!
I STAKED EVERY-THING ON THIS.
I PUT EVERYTHING I HAD INTO IT. AND YET...
shing
FATH-
...
DAD!
THERE'S STILL HOPE!
whap

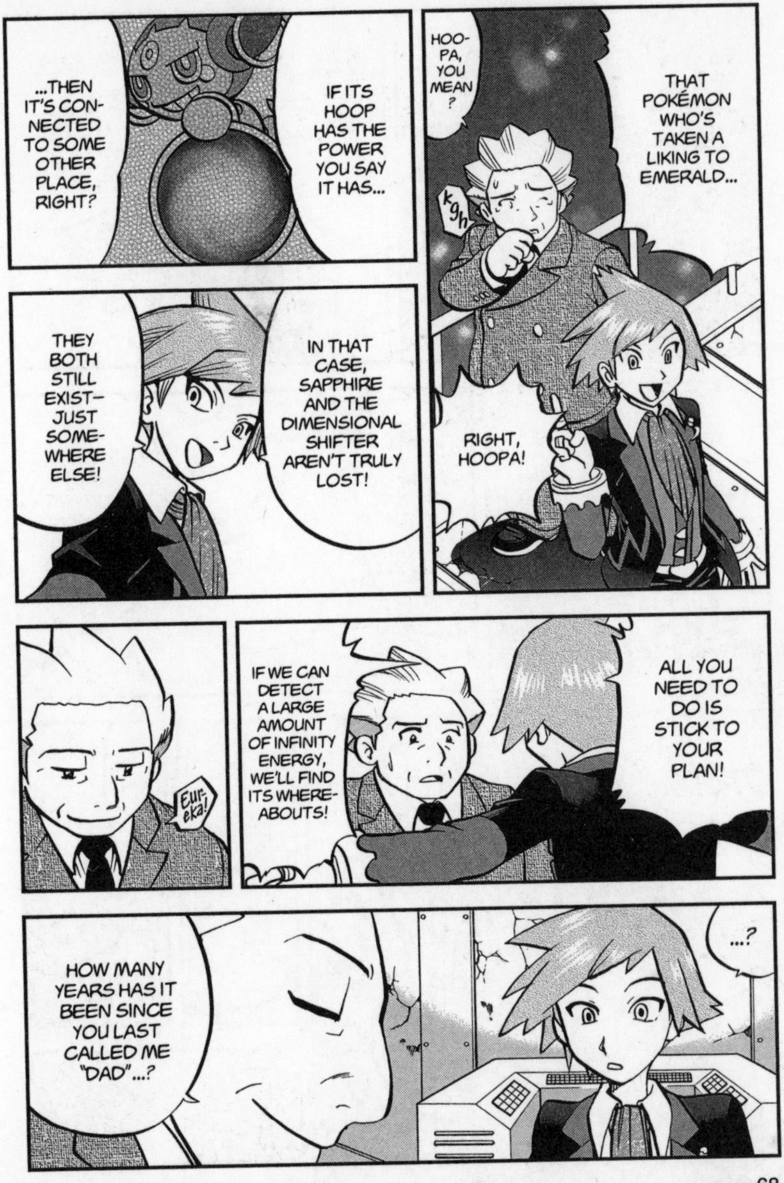
THAT POKÉMON WHO'S TAKEN A LIKING TO EMERALD...
HOO-PA, YOU MEAN?
kgh
IF ITS HOOP HAS THE POWER YOU SAY IT HAS...
...THEN IT'S CONNECTED TO SOME OTHER PLACE, RIGHT?
RIGHT, HOOPA!
IN THAT CASE, SAPPHIRE AND THE DIMENSIONAL SHIFTER AREN'T TRULY LOST!
THEY BOTH STILL EXIST—JUST SOMEWHERE ELSE!
ALL YOU NEED TO DO IS STICK TO YOUR PLAN!
IF WE CAN DETECT A LARGE AMOUNT OF INFINITY ENERGY, WE'LL FIND ITS WHEREABOUTS!
Eureka!
...?
HOW MANY YEARS HAS IT BEEN SINCE YOU LAST CALLED ME "DAD"...?

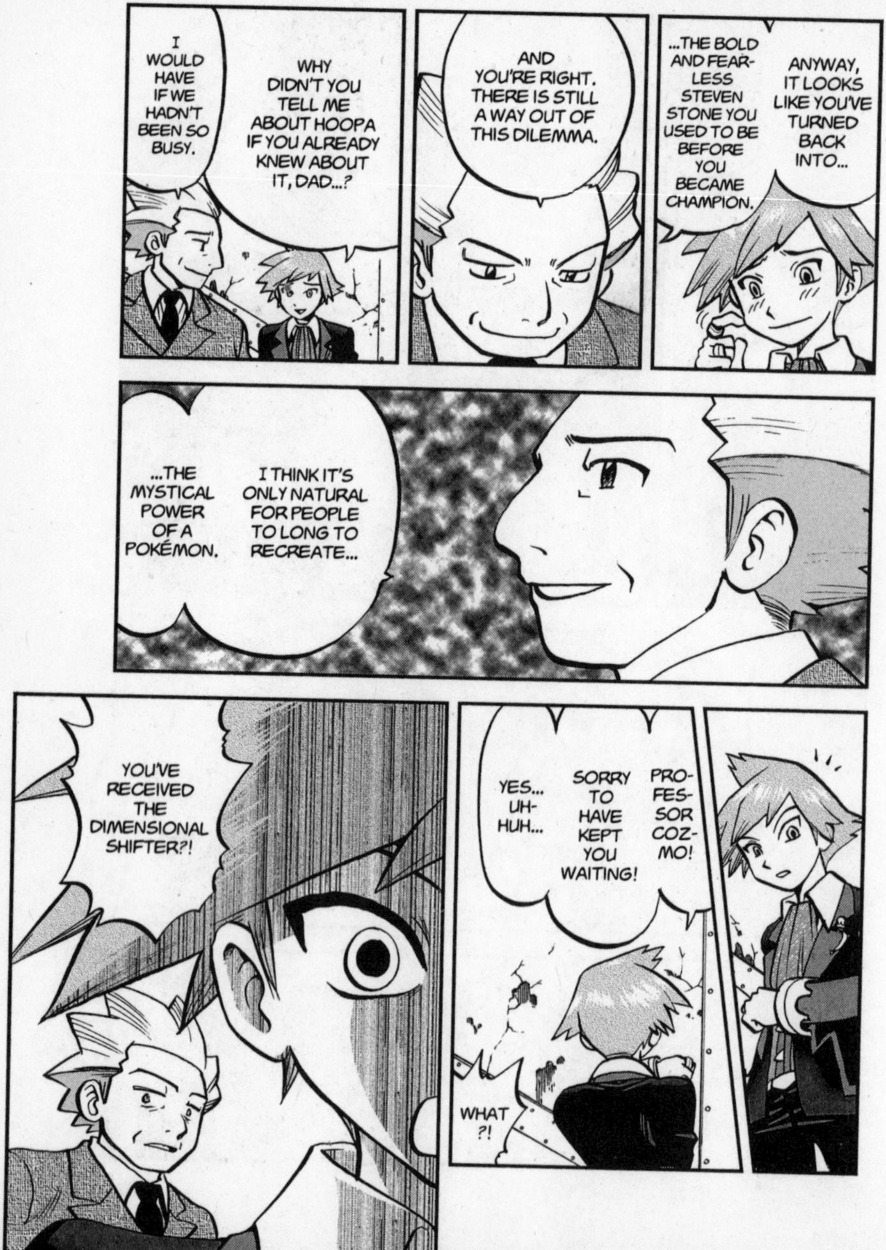
ANYWAY, IT LOOKS LIKE YOU'VE TURNED BACK INTO...
...THE BOLD AND FEAR-LESS STEVEN STONE YOU USED TO BE BEFORE YOU BECAME CHAMPION.
AND YOU'RE RIGHT. THERE IS STILL A WAY OUT OF THIS DILEMMA.
WHY DIDN'T YOU TELL ME ABOUT HOOPA IF YOU ALREADY KNEW ABOUT IT, DAD...?
I WOULD HAVE IF WE HADN'T BEEN SO BUSY.
I THINK IT'S ONLY NATURAL FOR PEOPLE TO LONG TO RECREATE...
...THE MYSTICAL POWER OF A POKÉMON.
PRO-FES-SOR COZ-MO!
SORRY TO HAVE KEPT YOU WAITING!
YES... UH-HUH...
WHAT ?!
YOU'VE RECEIVED THE DIMENSIONAL SHIFTER?!

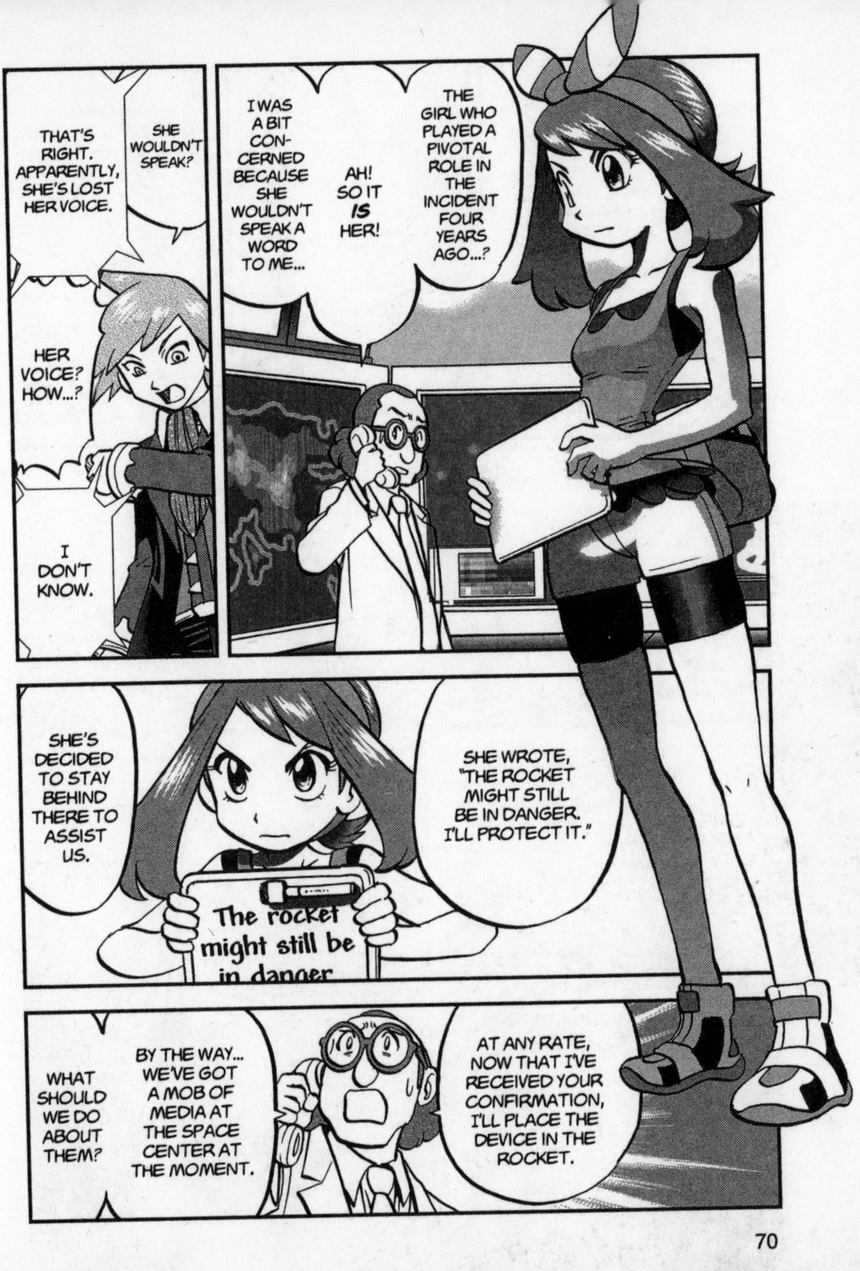
THE GIRL WHO PLAYED A PIVOTAL ROLE IN THE INCIDENT FOUR YEARS AGO...?
AH! SO IT *IS* HER!
I WAS A BIT CONCERNED BECAUSE SHE WOULDN'T SPEAK A WORD TO ME...
SHE WOULDN'T SPEAK?
THAT'S RIGHT. APPARENTLY, SHE'S LOST HER VOICE.
HER VOICE? HOW...?
I DON'T KNOW.
SHE WROTE, "THE ROCKET MIGHT STILL BE IN DANGER. I'LL PROTECT IT."
SHE'S DECIDED TO STAY BEHIND THERE TO ASSIST US.
The rocket might still be in danger
AT ANY RATE, NOW THAT I'VE RECEIVED YOUR CONFIRMATION, I'LL PLACE THE DEVICE IN THE ROCKET.
BY THE WAY... WE'VE GOT A MOB OF MEDIA AT THE SPACE CENTER AT THE MOMENT.
WHAT SHOULD WE DO ABOUT THEM?

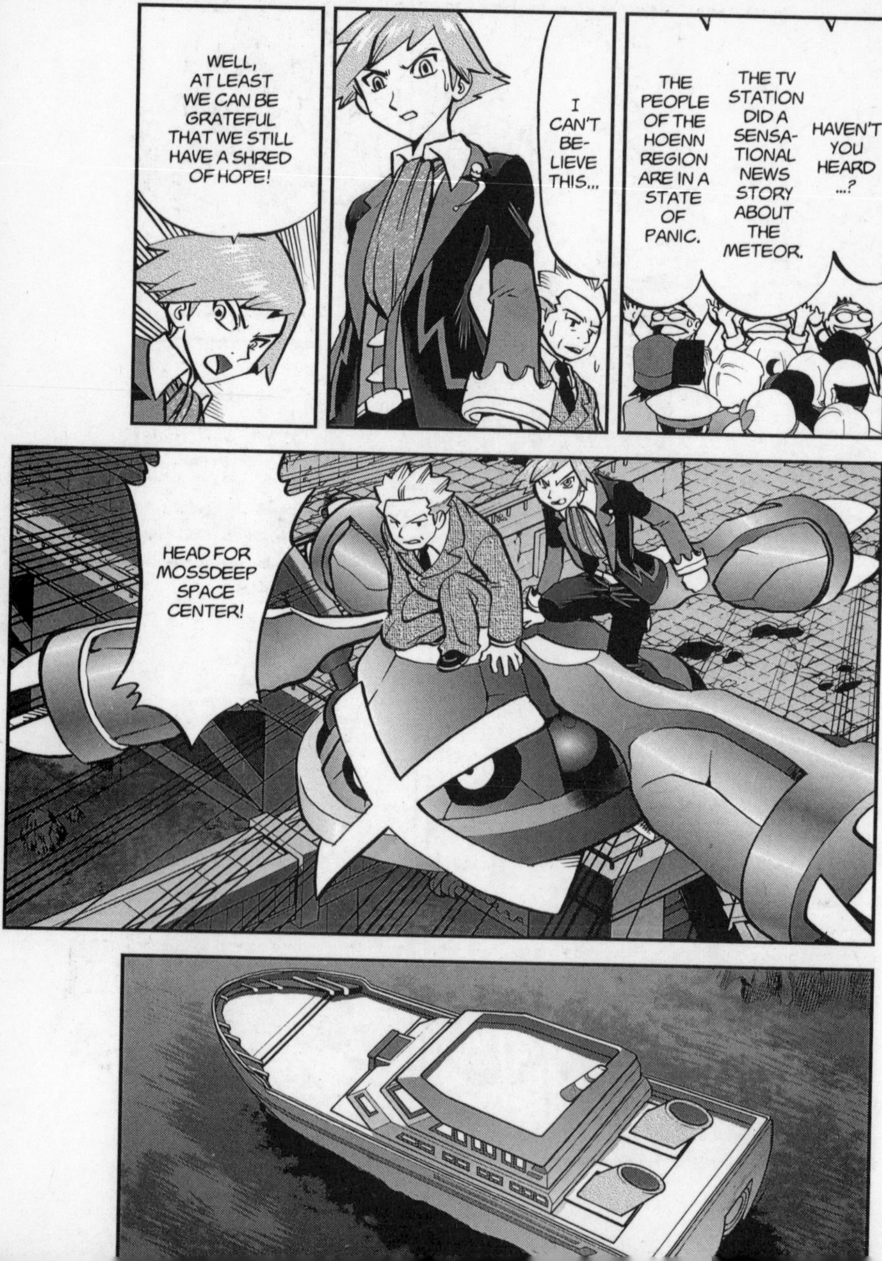
HAVEN'T YOU HEARD ...?
THE TV STATION DID A SENSA-TIONAL NEWS STORY ABOUT THE METEOR.
THE PEOPLE OF THE HOENN REGION ARE IN A STATE OF PANIC.
I CAN'T BE-LIEVE THIS...
WELL, AT LEAST WE CAN BE GRATEFUL THAT WE STILL HAVE A SHRED OF HOPE!
HEAD FOR MOSSDEEP SPACE CENTER!

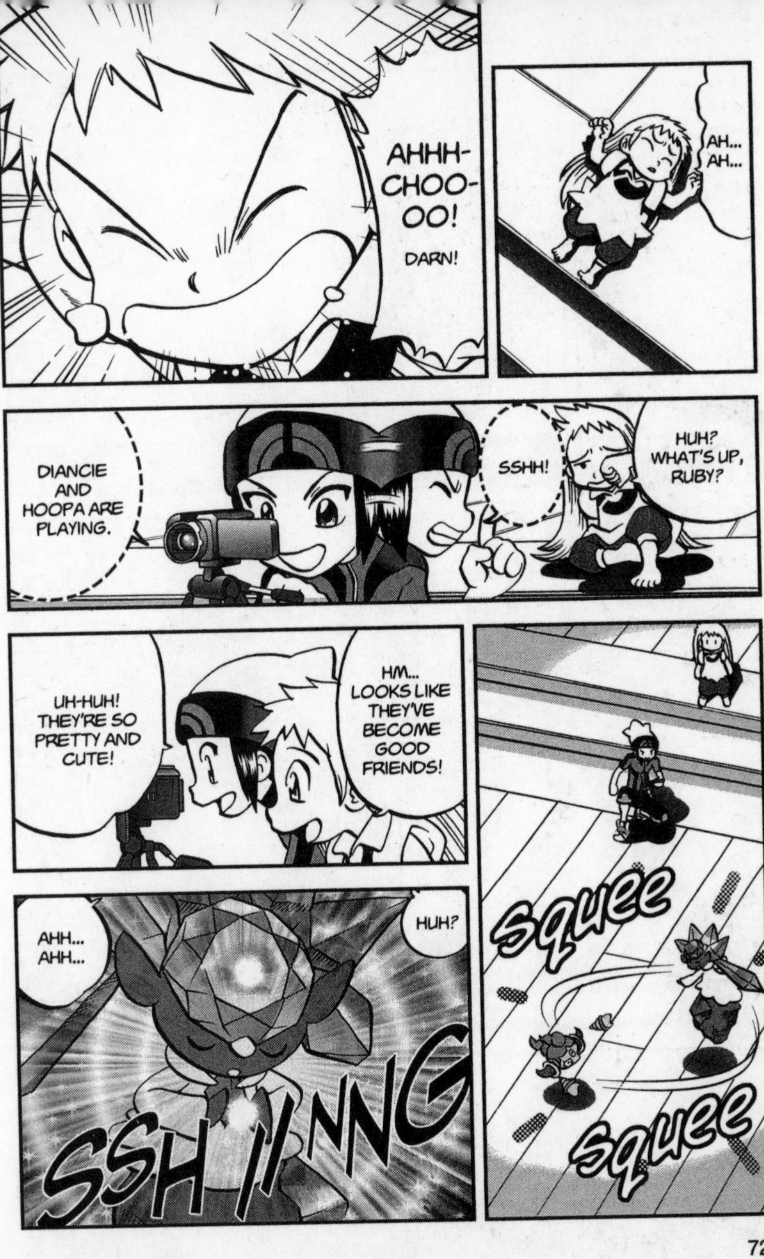
AH... AH...
AHHH-CHOOO-OO!
DARN!
HUH? WHAT'S UP, RUBY?
SSHH!
DIANCIE AND HOOPA ARE PLAYING.
squee
squee
HM... LOOKS LIKE THEY'VE BECOME GOOD FRIENDS!
UH-HUH! THEY'RE SO PRETTY AND CUTE!
HUH?
AHH... AHH...
SSHIINNG

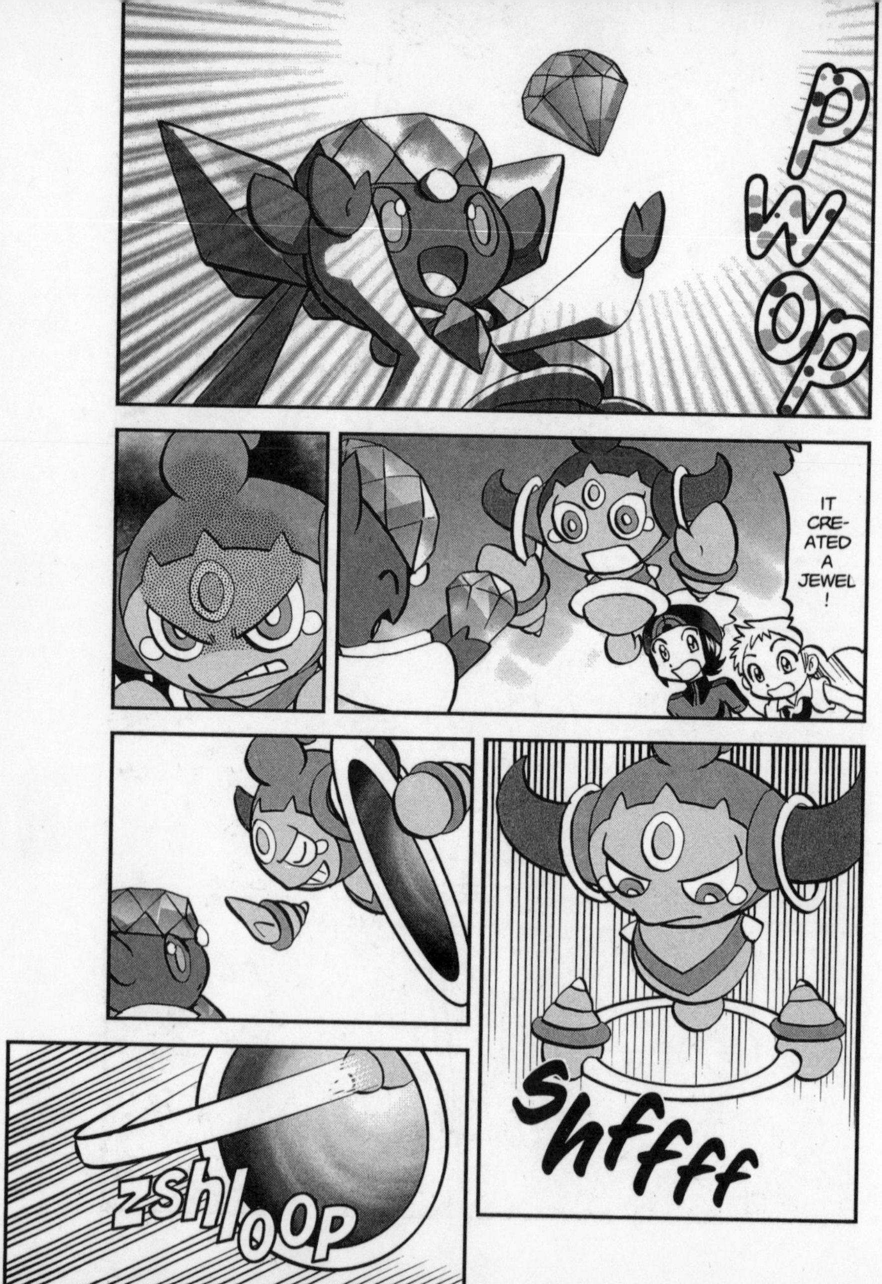
pwop
IT CRE-ATED A JEWEL!
Shffff
zshlOOP

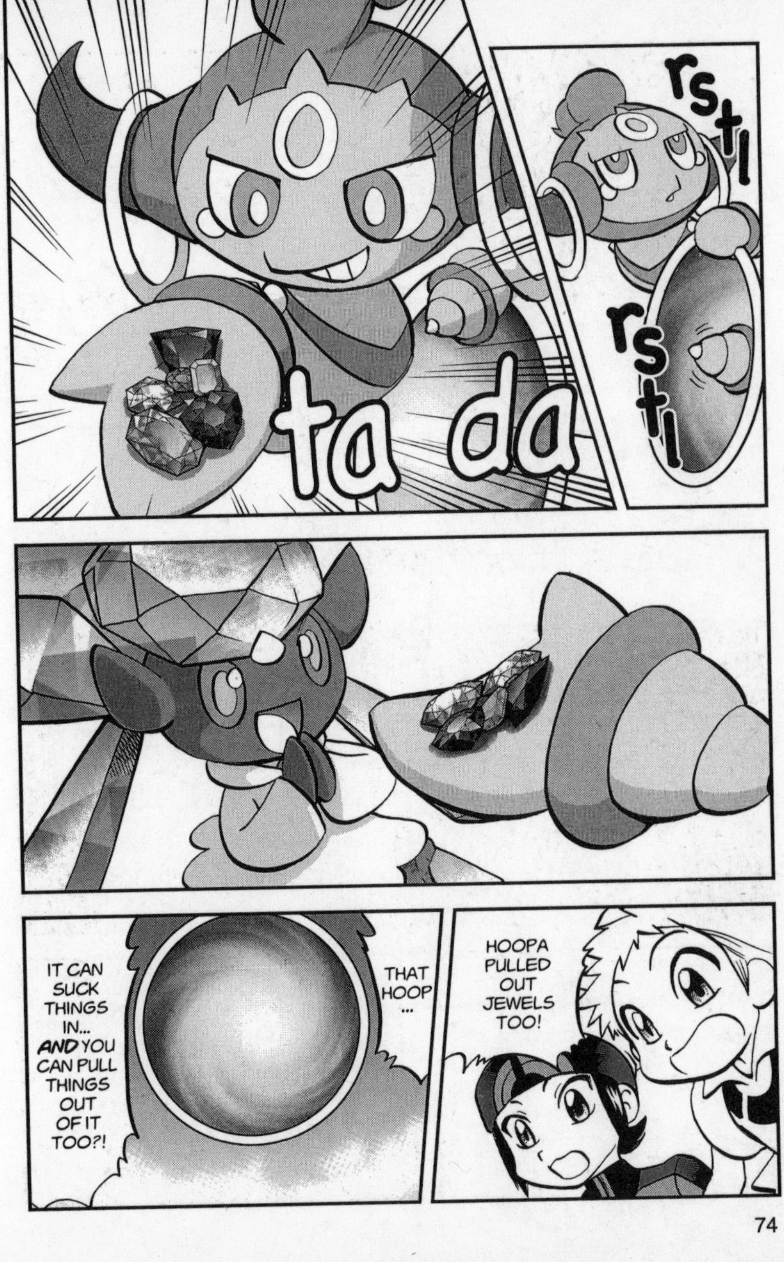
rstl
rstl
ta da
HOOPA PULLED OUT JEWELS TOO!
THAT HOOP...
IT CAN SUCK THINGS IN... **AND** YOU CAN PULL THINGS OUT OF IT TOO?!

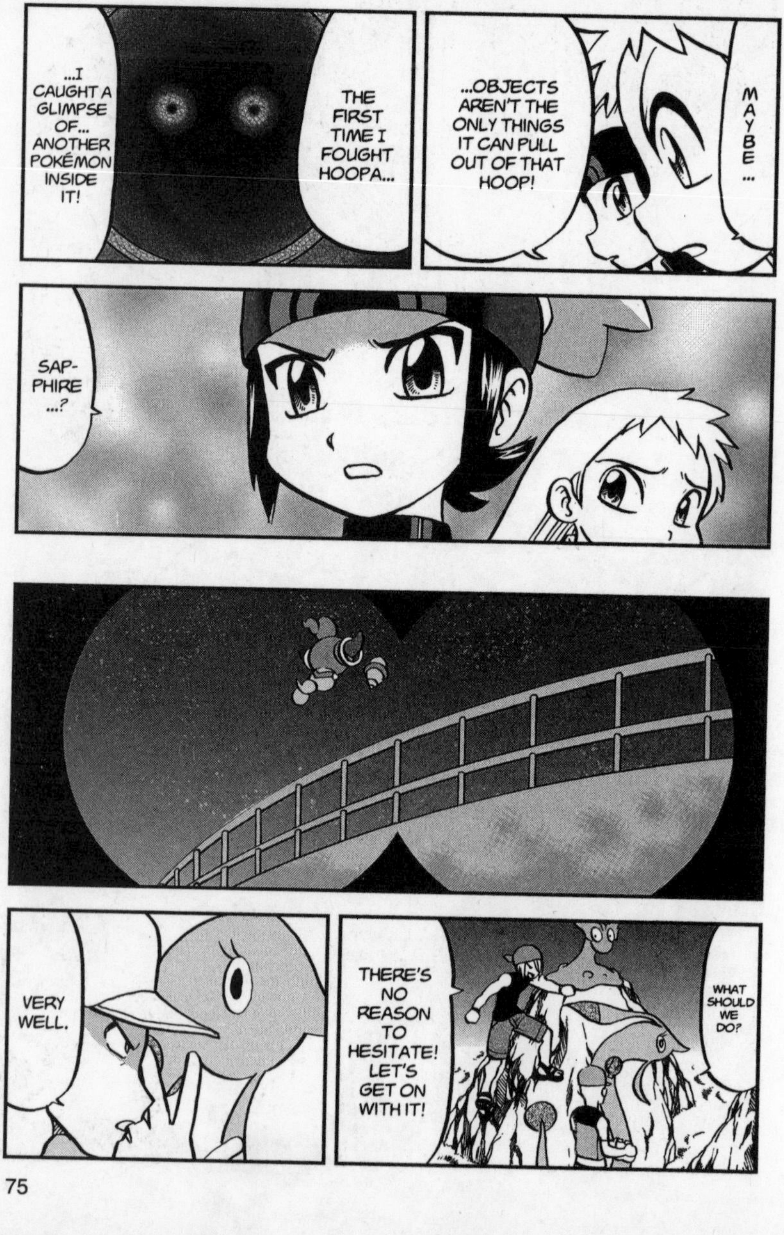
MAYBE...
...OBJECTS AREN'T THE ONLY THINGS IT CAN PULL OUT OF THAT HOOP!
THE FIRST TIME I FOUGHT HOOPA...
...I CAUGHT A GLIMPSE OF... ANOTHER POKÉMON INSIDE IT!
SAP-PHIRE...?
WHAT SHOULD WE DO?
THERE'S NO REASON TO HESITATE! LET'S GET ON WITH IT!
VERY WELL.

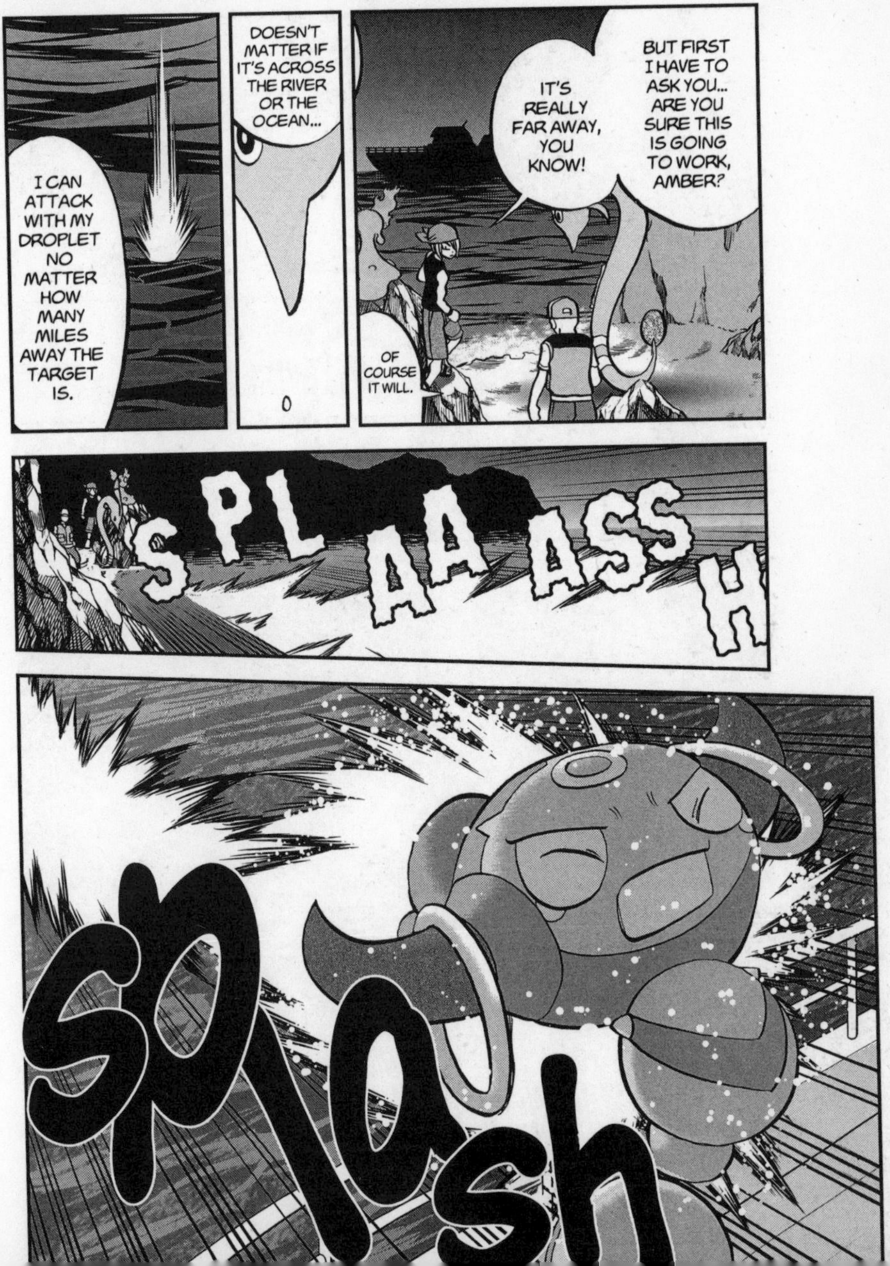
BUT FIRST I HAVE TO ASK YOU... ARE YOU SURE THIS IS GOING TO WORK, AMBER?
IT'S REALLY FAR AWAY, YOU KNOW!
OF COURSE IT WILL.
DOESN'T MATTER IF IT'S ACROSS THE RIVER OR THE OCEAN...
I CAN ATTACK WITH MY DROPLET NO MATTER HOW MANY MILES AWAY THE TARGET IS.
SPLAASSH
splash

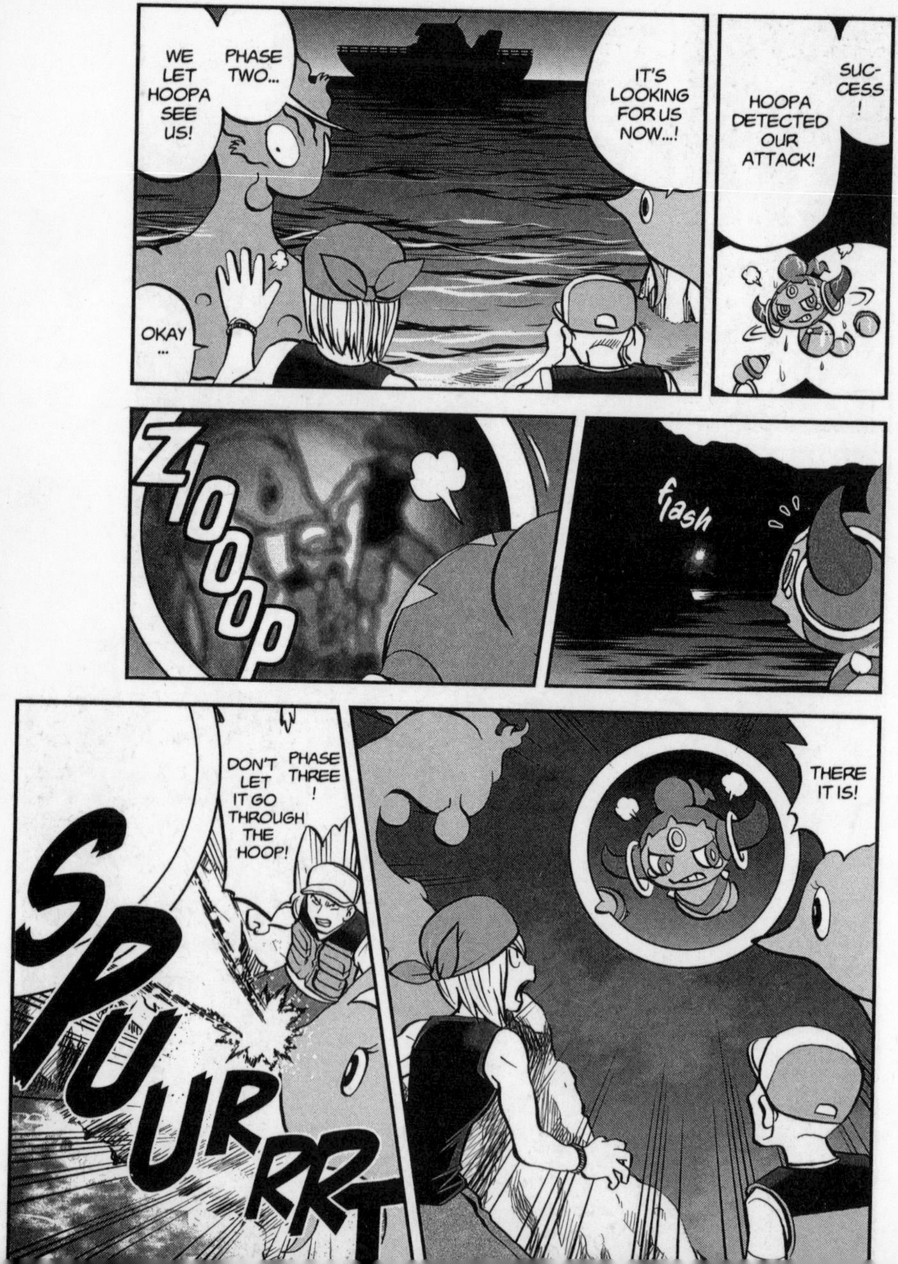
SUC-CESS!
HOOPA DETECTED OUR ATTACK!
IT'S LOOKING FOR US NOW...!
PHASE TWO...
WE LET HOOPA SEE US!
OKAY...
flash
ZIOOOOP
THERE IT IS!
PHASE THREE!
DON'T LET IT GO THROUGH THE HOOP!
SPUURRRT

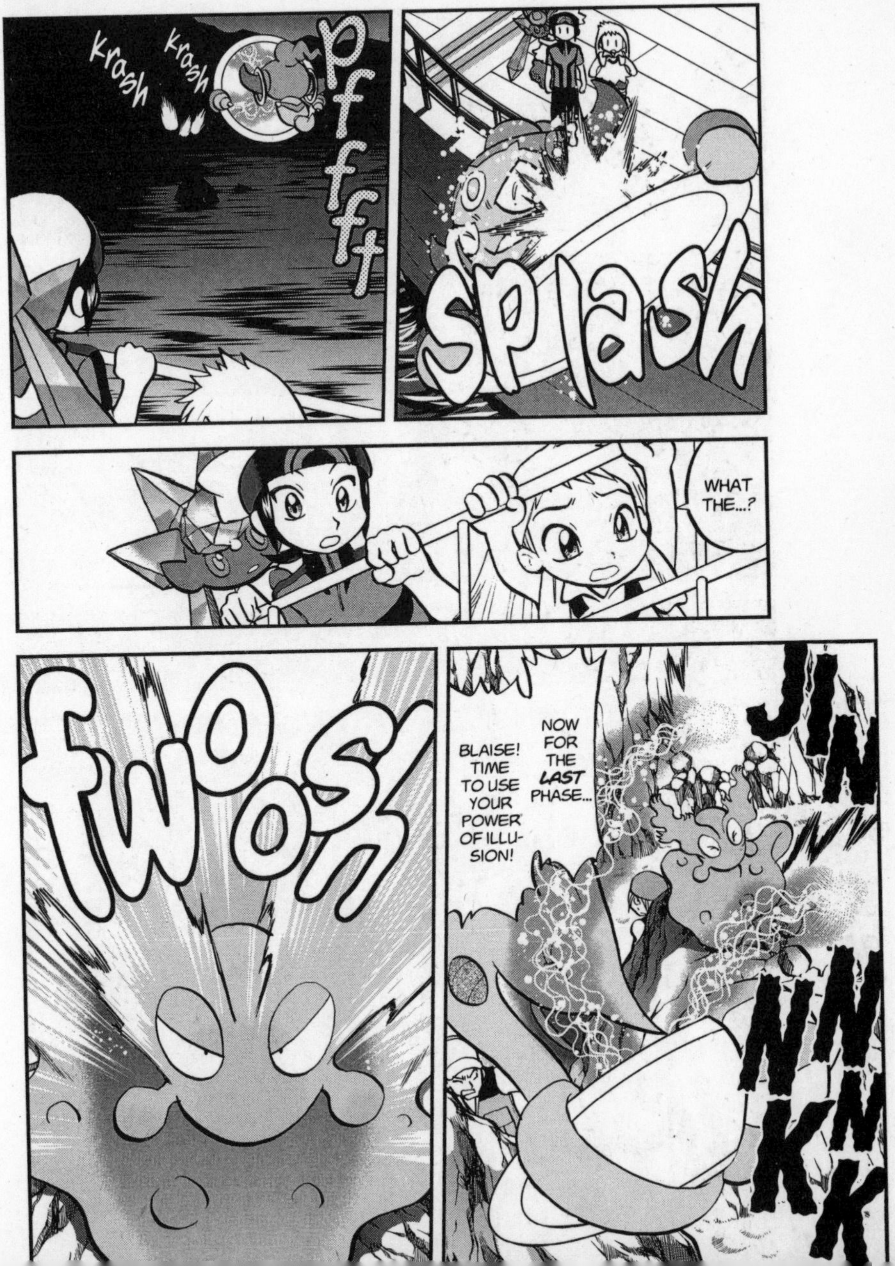
splash
krash
krash
pffffft
WHAT THE...?
JINNNNKK
NOW FOR THE LAST PHASE...
BLAISE! TIME TO USE YOUR POWER OF ILLUSION!
fwoosh

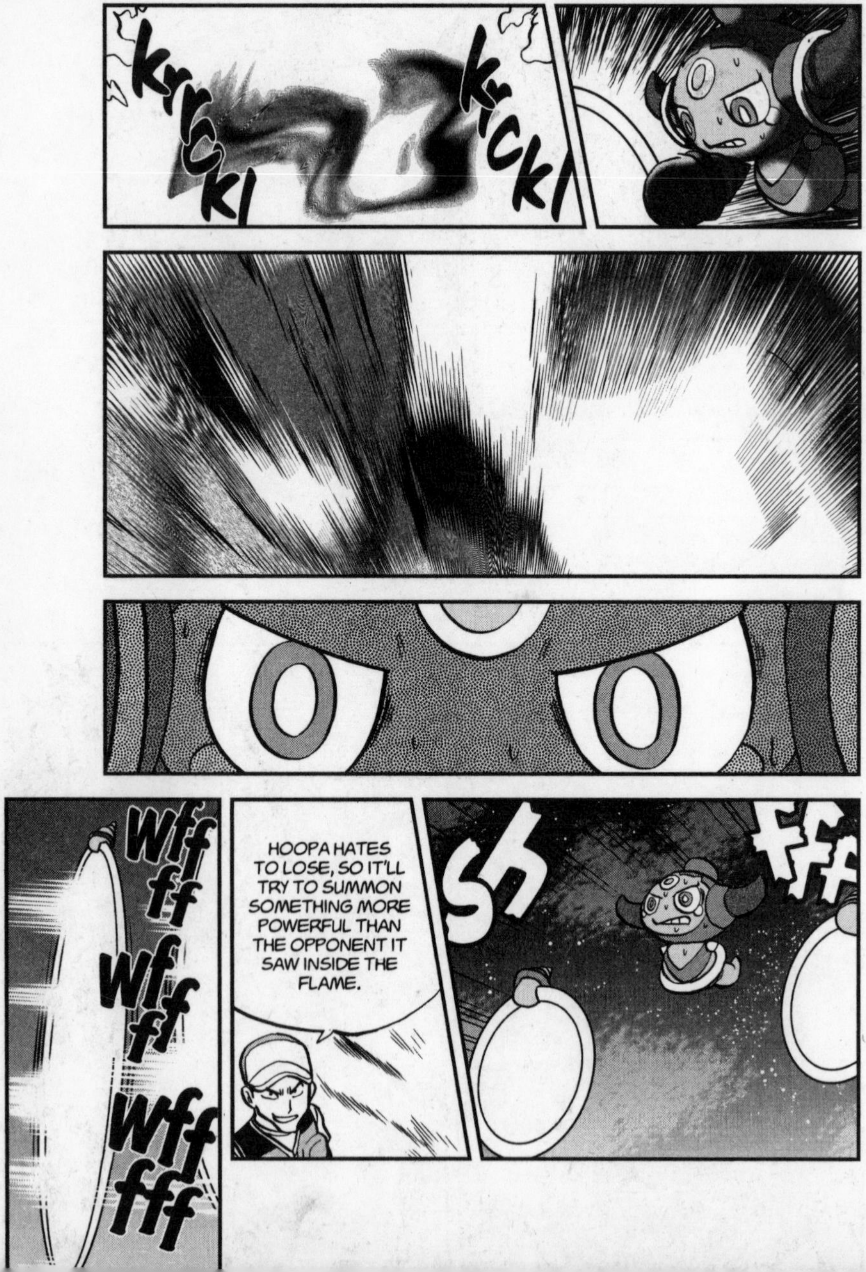
krrck!
krrck!
Sh
fff
HOOPA HATES TO LOSE, SO IT'LL TRY TO SUMMON SOMETHING MORE POWERFUL THAN THE OPPONENT IT SAW INSIDE THE FLAME.
wff ff
wff ff
wff fff

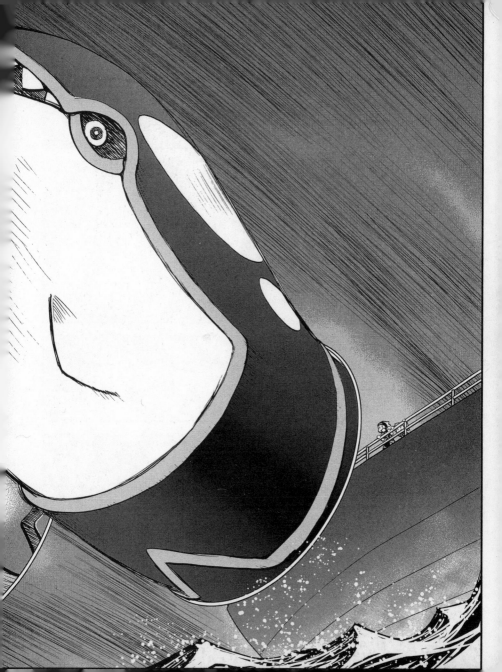

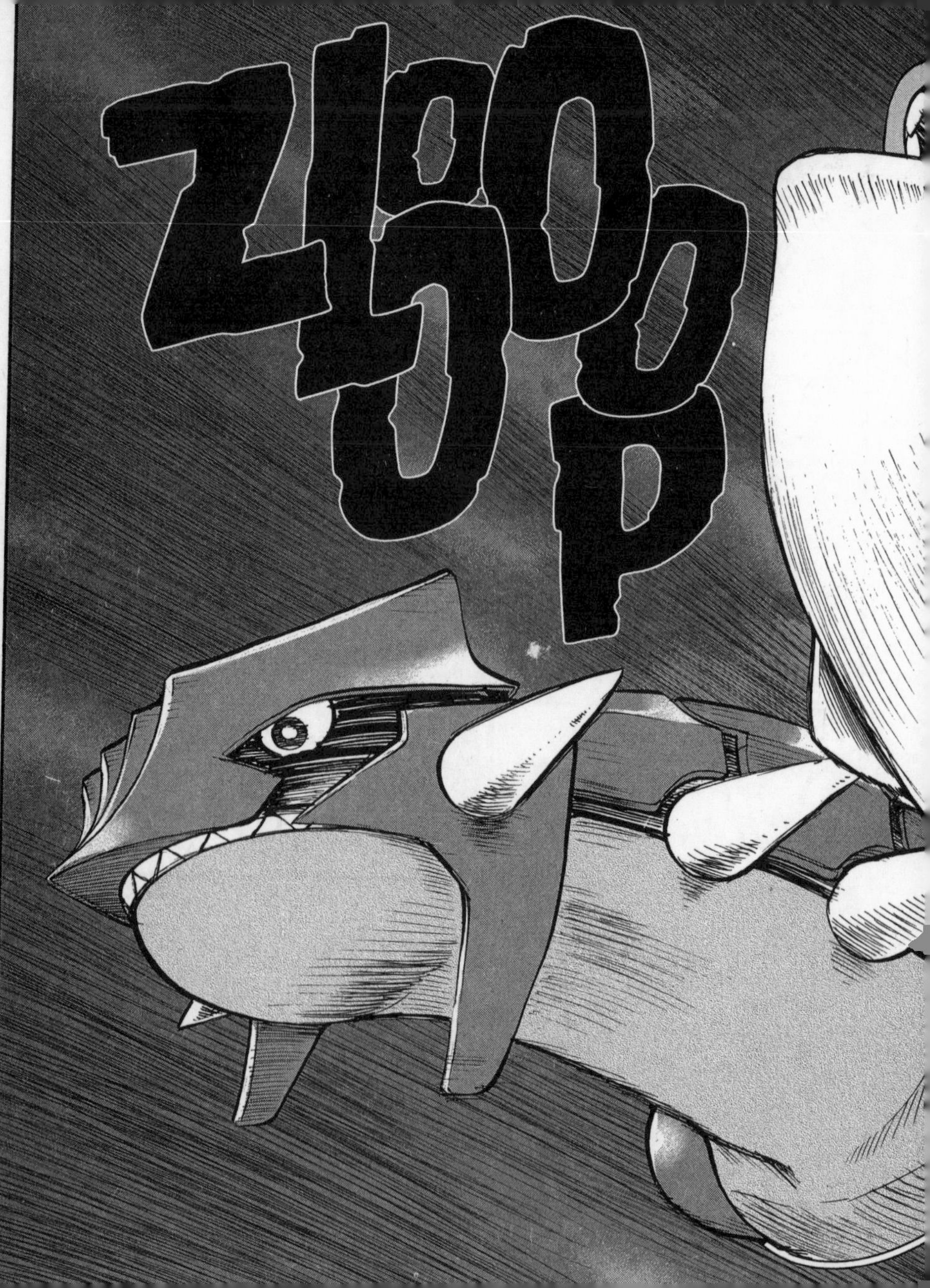

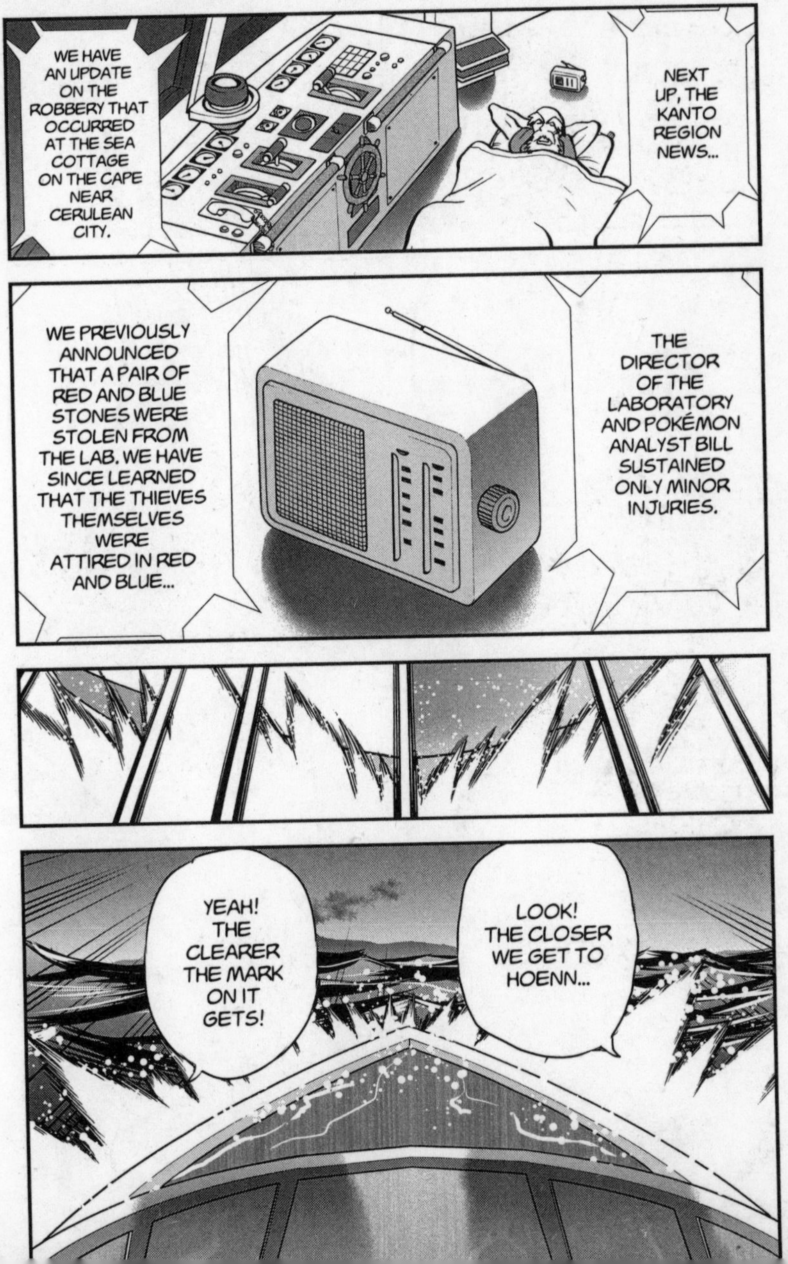
NEXT UP, THE KANTO REGION NEWS...
WE HAVE AN UPDATE ON THE ROBBERY THAT OCCURRED AT THE SEA COTTAGE ON THE CAPE NEAR CERULEAN CITY.
THE DIRECTOR OF THE LABORATORY AND POKÉMON ANALYST BILL SUSTAINED ONLY MINOR INJURIES.
WE PREVIOUSLY ANNOUNCED THAT A PAIR OF RED AND BLUE STONES WERE STOLEN FROM THE LAB. WE HAVE SINCE LEARNED THAT THE THIEVES THEMSELVES WERE ATTIRED IN RED AND BLUE...
LOOK! THE CLOSER WE GET TO HOENN...
YEAH! THE CLEARER THE MARK ON IT GETS!

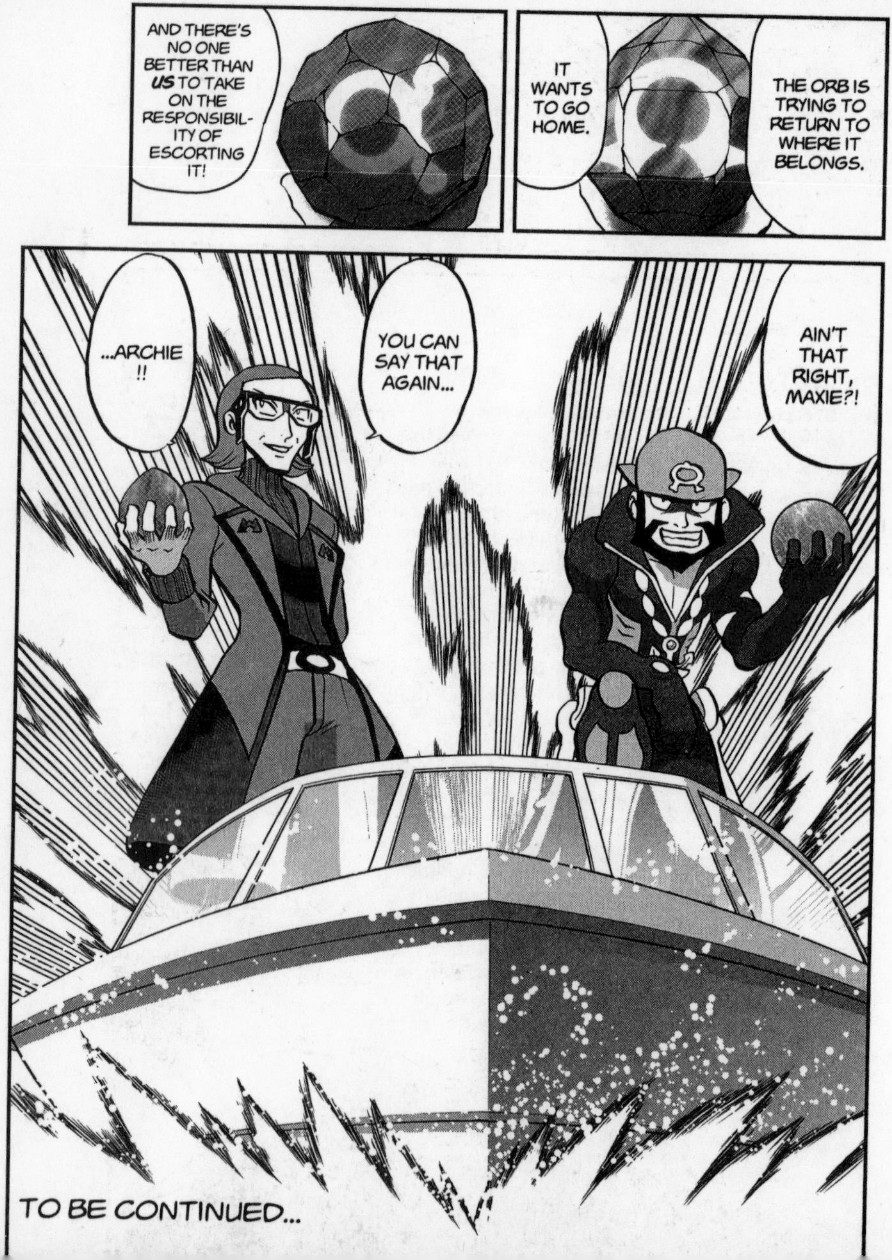
THE ORB IS TRYING TO RETURN TO WHERE IT BELONGS.
IT WANTS TO GO HOME.
AND THERE'S NO ONE BETTER THAN *US* TO TAKE ON THE RESPONSIBIL-ITY OF ESCORTING IT!
AIN'T THAT RIGHT, MAXIE?!
YOU CAN SAY THAT AGAIN...
...ARCHIE !!
TO BE CONTINUED...

PROJECT AZOTH

The name of the top secret operation in which the two ancient Pokémon were awoken.

GROUDON/KYOGRE

These two Legendary Pokémon are known as the Continent Pokémon and Sea Basin Pokémon. Legend has it that they are the personifications of the land and sea, so some researchers have concluded that they are the personification of Hoenn's natural environment. During ancient times, the two Pokémon often used to fight over the energy of nature. It is said that the battle between the two was halted by a Dragon-type Pokémon that flew out of the sky, but nothing further is known about the event. Groudon and Kyogre were awoken four years ago, and the clash between the two caused violent natural disasters in the region. They fell back into a deep slumber after the incident.

SEA COTTAGE

Bill is the manager of the Pokémon Storage System in the Kanto and Johto regions. He is also a Pokémon Analyst, and the Sea Cottage, which is located on the outskirts of Cerulean City, is where he takes care of his work. After the Deoxys incident the two cores of the orbs were kept at his place.

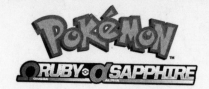

Pokémon ΩRuby • αSapphire
Volume 3
VIZ Media Edition

Story by HIDENORI KUSAKA
Art by SATOSHI YAMAMOTO

©2017 The Pokémon Company International.
©1995–2016 Nintendo/Creatures Inc./GAME FREAK inc.
TM, ®, and character names are trademarks of Nintendo.
POCKET MONSTERS SPECIAL ΩRUBY • αSAPPHIRE Vol. 2
by Hidenori KUSAKA, Satoshi YAMAMOTO
© 2015 Hidenori KUSAKA, Satoshi YAMAMOTO
All rights reserved.
Original Japanese edition published by SHOGAKUKAN.
English translation rights in the United States of America, Canada, the United
Kingdom, Ireland, Australia and New Zealand arranged with SHOGAKUKAN.

Translation—Tetsuichiro Miyaki
English Adaptation—Bryant Turnage
Touch-Up & Lettering—Susan Daigle-Leach
Design—Shawn Carrico
Editor—Annette Roman

The stories, characters and incidents mentioned
in this publication are entirely fictional.

Printed in the U.S.A.

Published by
VIZ Media, LLC
P.O. Box 77010
San Francisco, CA 94107

10 9 8 7 6 5 4 3 2 1
First printing, March 2017

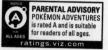

PARENTAL ADVISORY
POKÉMON ADVENTURES
is rated A and is suitable
for readers of all ages.
ratings.viz.com

www.viz.com

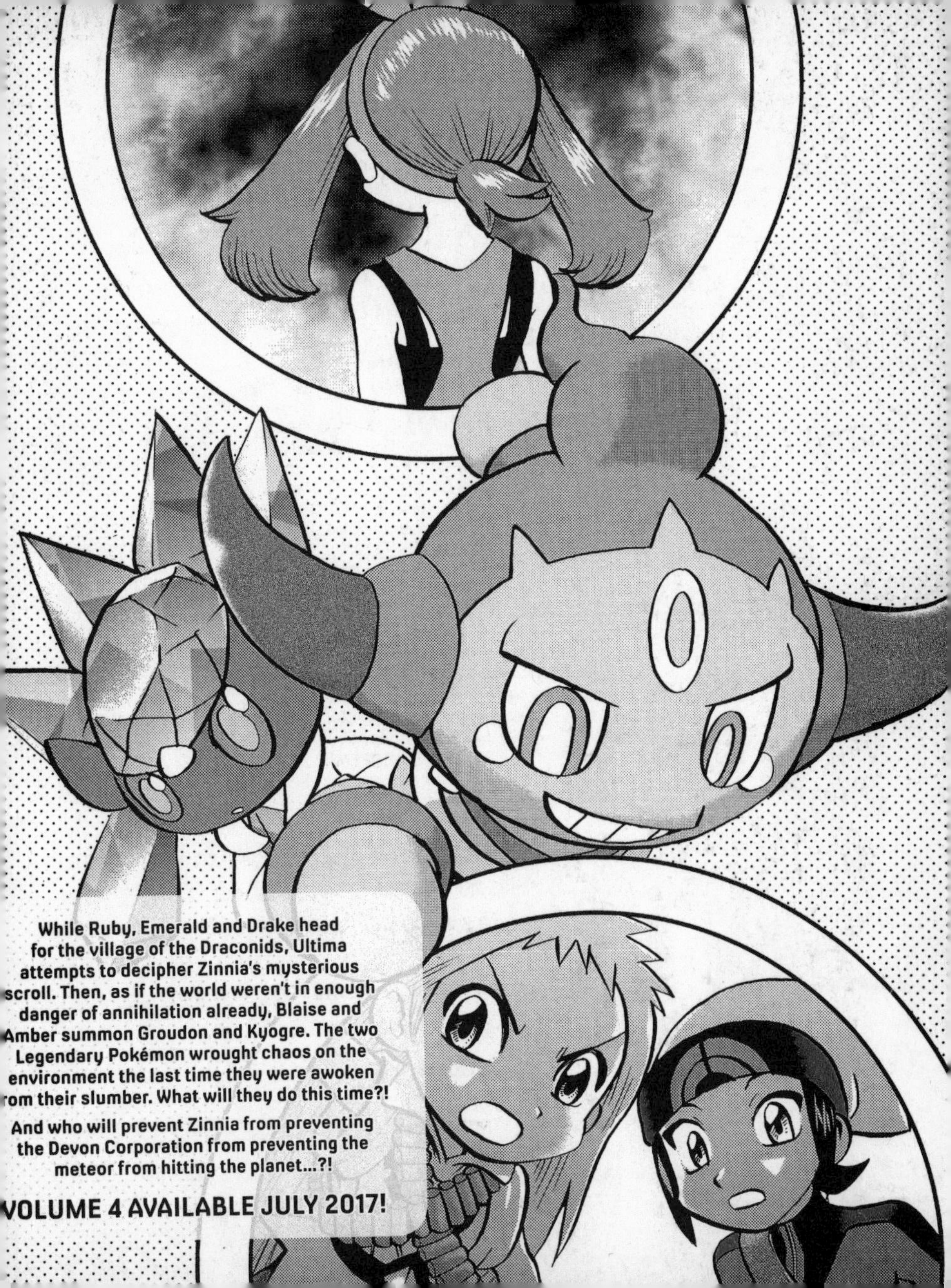
While Ruby, Emerald and Drake head for the village of the Draconids, Ultima attempts to decipher Zinnia's mysterious scroll. Then, as if the world weren't in enough danger of annihilation already, Blaise and Amber summon Groudon and Kyogre. The two Legendary Pokémon wrought chaos on the environment the last time they were awoken rom their slumber. What will they do this time?!
And who will prevent Zinnia from preventing the Devon Corporation from preventing the meteor from hitting the planet...?!
VOLUME 4 AVAILABLE JULY 2017!

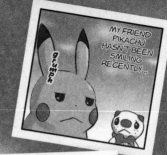
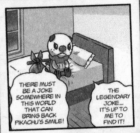
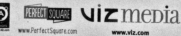
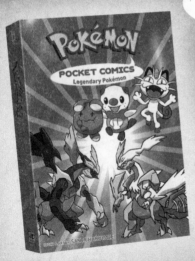

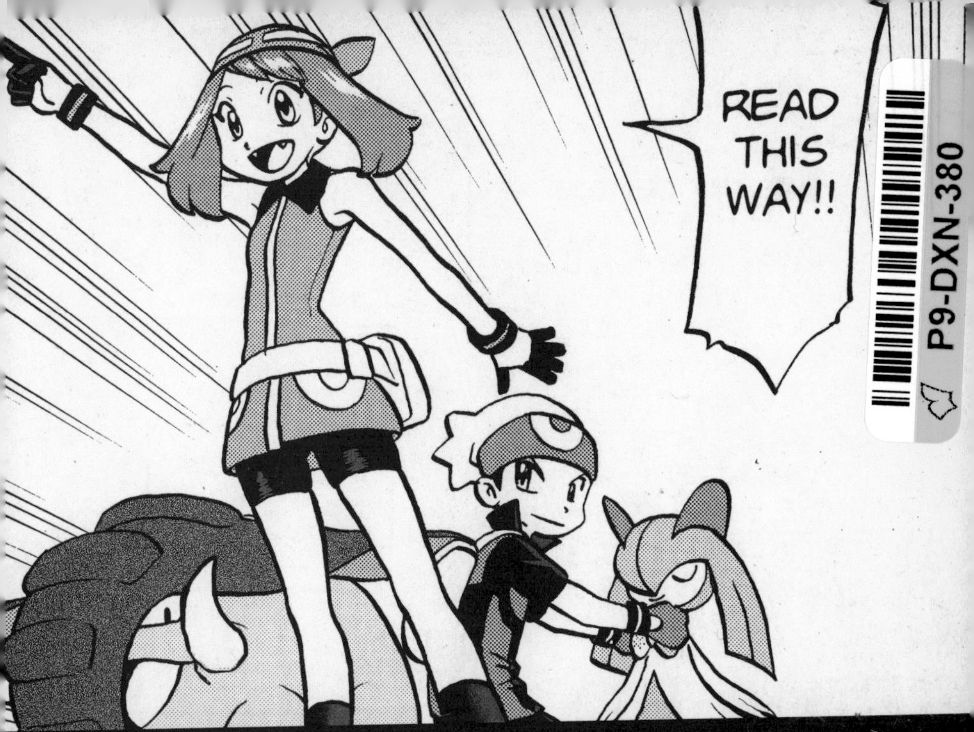
READ THIS WAY!!

THIS IS THE END OF THIS GRAPHIC NOVEL!

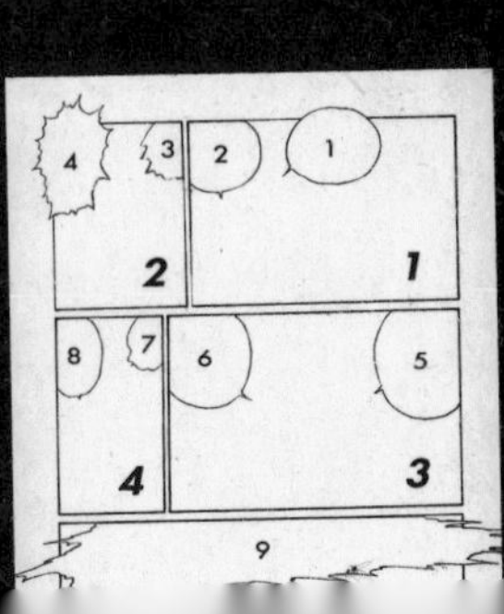

To properly enjoy this VIZ Media graphic novel, please turn it around and begin reading from right to left.

This book has been printed in the original Japanese format in order to preserve the orientation of the original